CAOLYN'S WISH

KARYN FINNERON

Published in the United States

ISBN 978-0-9857362-7-9

First edition 2020

Printed in the United States of America

1 2 3 4 5 6 7 8 9 10

Dedication

This book is dedicated to all those who still enjoy a bit of fantasy and adventure in difficult times. May you always have a wish in your heart and something to wish for in this world that has become so complicated.

I

The wise woman known as Cynara walked to the large oak door. In her heart, she knew this would be a difficult task; behind the door was a small, whimpering mass of sadness. The woman behind the door was no longer a maiden and not yet a crone, but she was on the path.

She had shown up at the wisewoman's door several nights before with tears streaming down her dirty face. Her hair was a mass of tangles and snarls, her clothes torn and dirty. The wisewoman had felt her coming long before she had arrived at her door. In preparation for Caolyn's coming Cynara had put the brewing pot on the fire and had thrown in a mixture of lavender flowers, along with skullcap and Melissa leaves. She knew that Caolyn would need relief from anxieties she had been experiencing of late, and Cynara was prepared to give her the brew as well as the reasons for drinking it. The tea would be strong, but if it gave the poor thing a night free of tossing, turning and worries, it would be worth it.

Caolyn had been named for the Goddess Caolainn because she was born at the time of the harvest. Harvest time was a time of celebration, preparation for the long winter which would follow, as well as a time for wishes for a bright new year. Cynara remembered the birthing day. It was the kind of warm and golden harvest day that almost makes one forget that soon the harshness of shorter days and frigid temperatures would be upon them.

When Cynara had looked at the beautiful new babe, she had known immediately that Caolyn would be chosen to follow the path. This beautiful girl child was born with auburn hair and amber eyes that could look into the soul of anyone who would cross her path. Her beautiful auburn hair also had a tiny streak of blond hair, shaped like a crescent moon, near her forehead. The mark of the Goddess was already on her tiny head. When Caolyn was given her name at the naming ceremony, all cheered, but Cynara did not. Cynara was just barely out of her maiden stage and beginning to be full with a new life of her own precious babe. She could see that naming the babe after Caolainn would come with a heavy burden as the babe matured.

Caolainn was the goddess of wishes and often wishes were granted that did not necessarily benefit the wisher. Caolainn often used the granted wish to teach the person a hard lesson in life. She was also a goddess to be called on for healing and fertility. These could involve wishes as well. This new babe would have to become well trained in the power of granting wishes and in understanding the power that wishes could hold.

All these thoughts were going through Cynara's mind as she prepared to open the door and tend to the young maid's needs. Perhaps Caolyn just needed the solace of being alone and perhaps the strong brew she had given her the night before had caused a restful and restorative sleep. Only opening the door could give the answer. With a gentle push, trying not to be too disturbing, Cynara opened the large oak door to the bed chamber.

It took Cynara a while for her old eyes to adjust to the darkness in the room. The morning had brought sun and clouds, but there were heavy drapes blocking the light from the windows. The room was like a tomb, dark, quiet and dank. It had been two days since Caolyn had come in the middle of the night. There were empty cups that had contained the strong tea that Cynara had left for the visitor. She walked into the room, choosing her steps carefully and quietly so as not to disturb the poor maid. As Cynara's eyes adjusted to the dark, she saw the young woman near the hearth, sleeping in a fetal position. The fire was nearly out and the room was cold. Cynara clutched her cloak closer as she moved toward the sleeping figure. She stopped, hesitated, and decided it would be best to get the fire in the hearth going first. Perhaps the warmth of the room would wake Caolyn and make her spirits rise.

While placing logs on the small embers and stoking the fire, Cynara could hear the stirring of the sleeping figure. "So, my sleeping lady, have you decided to come back among the waking, those that are alive?" Cynara asked. The curled-up heap began to stretch and rolled over towards the fire.

"How long have I been asleep, Auntie?" Caolyn asked.

"You have been with me nearly two days, my child. I did not want to disturb or impose upon you before you could have time to recoup your rest. I have never seen you as distraught as you were on your arrival."

Caolyn sat up and looked around the room and then lay back down on the blankets spread on the floor.

Cynara continued to stoke the fire. She was waiting for some word, some explanation from the young woman. She was trying to be patient, trying to rely on the wisdom that comes with age and wait until the younger woman was ready to speak. "How I would like to go to her and pull the words from her mouth with a speaking spell," Cynara thought, "but no, I will wait a bit longer."

Cynara moved toward the window and began to pull back the drapes. "PLEASE, NO!" Caolyn screamed. "I am too horrible a creature in my present state. Please don't look at me, Auntie," Caolyn begged.

"My dear child, I saw you at your worst when you stumbled on my doorstop two days ago. Surely you are no worse. Perhaps it is your wounded spirit that you feel is ugly. It may be better for you to speak and release your worries and fears."

When Caolyn sat up and faced her "auntie," Cynara could see that the young woman had cried long and hard. The only clean places on her soiled face were the tracks of the tears that had been cried until no tears were left. Cynara thought, "She must have hurt herself or someone else to their very soul to have cried so much." Aloud she began, "Perhaps, my girl, you should try to some of your heart on me. There is little I have not heard or seen by this time in my life. You cannot surprise me with words or feelings that I most likely have even experienced."

"Auntie," began Caolyn, "you have known me forever and you know that in my heart I would never willingly hurt another person or creature, but I fear that by trying to help a friend, I have not only hurt her but myself and, perhaps, an innocent third person as well."

Cynara could see that the young woman was struggling to find the words. She patiently waited while

Caolyn herself. Looking into her young face barely out of maidenhood, Cynara saw how much Caolyn looked like her mother, Myra. Myra had been Cynara's closest friend. They had been chosen to learn the way of the Great Mother and together they had gone to the chapel of the Lady by the Great Lake to study. Myra had the special gift of being able to sense the feelings of others. She could look at a person and almost instantly know if the person was of a good or evil nature, happy or suffering deep sorrow, healthy or sick in body, mind or spirit. She had a way of reading people and the earth that could compare to no other. She had been taken from this earth far too soon. She had been mortally wounded when a tribe of evil warriors tried to cross the Great Lake to pillage and attack the School of Maidens.

Cynara was shaken from her thoughts by Caolyn's voice. "Auntie, are you listening?"

"Yes, my child, forgive my distraction. At times my old mind wanders to a different time. Go on."

"Auntie, remember Brenna from the village of Breac, daughter of the Chieftain?"

"Yes, my dear, go on."

"Brenna had come into maidenhood at the last celebration of Beltane and she desires one of the young warriors in her village. She asked if I would bring her wish to the Goddess Caolainn for whom I am named. Her wish is to have the warrior from the village become her beloved." Caolyn's voice broke and she stopped in the middle of the story. Cynara waited for her to begin again, but her senses told her that Caolyn might have prayed to the Goddess to grant a beloved to a friend when Caolyn had wanted the young warrior for herself.

Caolyn composed herself and began again. "I met the

warrior known as Ronan at the same Beltane feast as did Brenna. He was so fair of face and so beautiful. He was swimming in the small pond by the grove of hawthorn trees. I watched him quietly for some time. He is a very powerful swimmer, and I later learned from some of the other warriors that the Chieftain often sends him into the water at night in order for him to get close to enemy boats and listen for their secrets of battle. He is trusted by the Chieftain."

Cynara could see by the light in the young maiden's eyes and hear in her voice that she had truly been smitten with this young warrior. When the fires of Beltane were lit and a young maiden is ready, it did not take much for the heart to start its longing. "Go on my dear, I am listening."

"I felt I could not continue to stare at him out of respect for his person, but I also felt my heard pounding as it had never done before. I knew that before this night was over, I had to find a way to speak with him. I have no brother and I never knew who my father was, so I could not see a way to a proper introduction."

"My dear Caolyn, when a girl has come into her maidenhood, and is without a father or a brother to offer an introduction to a young man, the next best person is one of the wise women or crones of the village. Surely, you could have come to me, and I would have guided you through a proper introduction."

"I know, Auntie," Caolyn began, "but I got so distracted by the feasting at Beltane and the night seemed to pass so quickly. I knew that Ronan had not been chosen that night by another maiden because I heard the young warriors all teasing each other about which one of them would choose this maiden or that.

Ronan seemed to be holding back and not offering any information. His friend, Bel, with hair as red as flames, was playfully taunting Ronan saying because he swam with the fish and seals, he had no time for the women of the land. He would rather seek out a sea siren. They were all laughing in good humor, so I took that to mean he had not yet found a maiden to seek out. Before I knew it, it was time for the Circle of Fire, and all of us who had newly come into maidenhood, planned to be together at the Fire. Unless, of course, they had found some handsome young man to spend time with at the celebration. I found Brenna alone, as was I, so together we went to the Fire."

"So, you had missed your opportunity to meet this young man who had caught your eye?"

"Yes, Auntie, but I did not think that my opportunity had passed me by all together. I felt that soon with the summer season on us and more gatherings of people in the outdoors that I would have an opportunity to meet him," Caolyn continued.

"One must seek the opportunity as it presents itself, my child. The Goddess often gives us but one moment of precious time to use before the gift of chance is gone. But come, let me fix you something to eat while you take care to cleanse and freshen yourself. Everything always seems worse when we are not pleased with our own sense of self. One cannot feel well when one is so rumpled and one's clothes have not been refreshed."

"But, Auntie," Caolyn began.

Cynara raised her hand, "Enough, my child, trust my wisdom and the time I have spent walking paths you have not yet crossed. I will listen to your story once you have bathed and put on fresh garments. Then you shall nourish your body and I will listen to your dilemma. Together we will find a way to make things right once I hear your story. Now off with you! I will be in the hearth room preparing food to break our fast and then I will listen."

"I will do as you say, Auntie but......" Caolyn began. Cynara only raised her hand again and started towards the door. Caolyn knew that meant for now the conversation was ended.

II

B ack in the hearth room, Cynara stoked the fire and added a log to the glowing embers. "What could be so disruptive to this maiden's mind? She seems to be disturbed to her very core," Cynara thought. She moved about the room taking food stuffs from the shelves and placing a kettle on the fire. "Chamomile tea with lavender and honey will calm her soul as well as mine. Heaven only knows what a tangled mess can happen when young love and jealousies mix. Some days I miss being a young maid, all those thoughts of love and feelings for some young handsome warrior." As her eyes misted over, she spoke aloud. "Oh, but I would not want to go through the pain of loss that for me came with the love I had for my Bran!" After all these years, the pain is at times still so great, as if it were only a fortnight ago."

Cynara had always been an earnest student in the House of Maidens. Early on in her studies she knew that the making of potions and teas, as well as healing salves for wounds, was where her strength lay. She also learned that she had almost a natural feel for what medicinal plants could be used to help with battle wounds, childbirth pains. Now that she had reached wisewoman status, she could help the elders with the pains associated with age and ease their journey to the next world with calming scents and blessing oils. "Yes, it is good not to have the emotions of the young anymore," she thought; "and yet here I am dealing with Caolyn. We shall see what can be done for her, but first she must be calm enough to speak her mind."

Caolyn was like her own child because, after the loss of her one and only babe at birth and then the loss of Bran, taking care of Caolyn had been a blessing. Bran had gone off to battle to defend the village against a warring tribe to the north and suffered mortal wounds. This was shortly after the loss of her babe, and so great was her grief that she threw herself into her study of plants and taking care of the health of the members of their village. Over time, she found her way through the grief by giving to others, but there were always the days when it came rushing back.

Then Myra, Caolyn's mother and Cynara's closest friend at the House of Maidens, came to her and announced to Cynara that she believed she was with child. "How happy I was for her," Cynara thought. Myra had found her beloved and she had been to the Lady Ava to tell her of her love. Soon there would be a Hand Fasting Ceremony for them. Cynara remembered teasing Myra that she had not shared her beloved's name with her best friend. Myra had confessed that she did not share the name because he was from a neighboring village and wanted to learn more about him before making his name known. He had come with several companions from his village to a festival, and he had seen Myra there. Myra shared the story of how, on the first night of the festival, she had danced with the visitor and they both share a few glasses of mead with him. With that information Cynara had scolded Myra, saying that the young women studying the ways of the Goddess had been instructed to abstain or at least be careful around drinking festivities.

Thinking of this now, Cynara became saddened. The mead surely would have compromised Myra's abilities to judge the visitor in a proper light. But then, the heart wants what it seeks, and the two young people spent the night locked in the charms of each other. When Myra discovered herself with child, she had her brother seek him out, but when her brother Drest returned, he told Myra her heart's desire was pledged to another. Drest was enraged and anger spewed from his mouth when telling of how he found Bain, her "fine young man!" Not only was he pledged to another, but there was also a family, a wife and a young boy. The wife, like Myra, was also full with new life, and soon she would have a new babe. Drest swore vengeance. Myra forbid him to seek any retribution. To have taken Bain's life would change nothing, and it would have left a distraught widow and fatherless children. She could not live with this, and it would not change the fact that she would still be with child.

Broken in spirit, Myra went to Ava, the Lady of the House of Maidens, and told her of her plight. Ava advised Myra that the babe would be loved by the maidens who were childless, and if it were a boy, they would foster him out when the time came. The House would be no place for a boy child who would need the presence of a man in his life.

Then there had been the raid on the House of Maidens by a warring, neighboring village. The warriors from the village sworn to protect the House were away practicing their war skills with other warriors, and as a result, arrived late to the raid. Fortunately, there was not much damage to the House and the store of sacred, healing herbs and medicinal plants. However, several of the very young maidens had been killed or taken away as hostages. Myra, big with child, could not get to cover quickly and was severely wounded, but alive. Once the raid had ended and the damage had been assessed, Cynara was called to attend the wounded including her friend Myra. It was clear the wounds were bringing about the start of the birthing ritual.

Cynara was there for the birthing and eased Myra's pains with birthing herbs and salves to rub on her swollen belly. Myra's labor was long and difficult and her having been wounded did not ease the situation. After a full day of agony, the girl babe burst forth from Myra's body. She was beautiful and crying vigorously. Cynara put the babe to Myra's breast and the baby latched on with the strength of a hungry pup.

Cynara attended to Myra and the baby. The baby was doing well but Myra seemed to be getting weaker. Despite strong teas, fresh milk from the cows, and thick porridges fed to Myra, there did not seem to be any real improvement. The naming ceremony was being planned for the seventh day after the birth. Cynara was hoping that Myra would be healthy by then. It had been decided to name the babe Caolainn in honor of the Goddess of Wishes. Cynara's wish was that that Myra would be made well.

On the night before the naming ceremony, Myra called Cynara to her side and tearfully told her friend that she knew she was dying. Cynara would not hear of it! She implored her friend to fight on, but in her heart, she knew her friend was not getting stronger, but rather visibly fading away. "Promise me, Cynara, you will take care of my daughter. She can live with you in the House of Maidens, promise." Cynara nodded her head.

"I have seen the Banshee in my dreams; I have heard her wailing on the nights I cannot sleep," Myra said. "I am not afraid; I am ready and I will rest easy knowing that you will care for my daughter. I feel I will make the naming ceremony, but my time grows short."

Cynara's eyes filled with tears over with the memory of the beautiful naming ceremony. That night Caolyn was brought to Myra. "I would like to try to feed her," Myra said. Cynara gently put the baby to breast and after a few short moments, Myra closed her eyes and smiled for the last time.

Cynara was pushed from her memories by the sound of footsteps. "Auntie," began Caolyn, "I found some old robes in one of the chests in the bed chamber. They are old but do not seem worn. I hope you don't mind. As you know, I came with nothing and my things are so dirty."

Cynara turned and almost fell over but caught herself. "AUNTIE! Are you all right?!" Caolyn exclaimed rushing towards the old woman.

"I, I, I'm fine my dear, it is just that seeing you in that dress….," Cynara began.

"I'm sorry. Auntie. I should have asked your permission first. Do you want me to change?"

"No dear, it is just that I was remembering things gone past and seeing you in that, it was your mother's you know and you seem so much like her now that you are grown," Cynara explained.

"This was my mother's?! It is beautiful. It must have been for something special," Caolyn began.

"It was my dear; she wore it to a festival on the night

that you became a tiny seedling growing within her. She looked beautiful that night, and it was no wonder any young man would find her attractive, as they would if they were to see you."

With that statement, Caolyn sat down and her mood changed back to one of sadness. You could see the dark veil of an unhappiness settling in the room.

Cynara was quick to go to the hearth, and pour a cup of lavender and chamomile tea for the girl, and to bring her some fresh berries and newly made bread. "Now my girl, you shall eat and then we shall begin to discover what makes your heart and spirit so sad. As I have said, there is little I have never heard. Together, we will try to find a solution to your problem."

"Thank you, Auntie; shall I say the blessing words?"

"Yes, my child, begin.

"Great Mother, we thank you for the food before us, the friends beside us, and the love between us," Caolyn said reverently.

The women began their simple meal and once finished settled down together. "So Caolyn, speak about what is troubling you," Cynara began. She noticed that the young maiden was much more at ease than she had been earlier. "Rest, food and cleanliness nourishes body and soul," Cynara thought.

Caolyn began her story. "As I have said Auntie, Brenna asked me to help her find favor with a young warrior from the village. I asked her why she needed me to help as she is the Chieftain's daughter, and as such, her sire could arrange any meeting with any number of favorable young men in the village and beyond. Brenna wanted the young man she had chosen to find favor with her first, and then perhaps, ask her father for her hand. I told her that I could do a wishing spell, but that the Goddess Caolainn grants only certain wishes. The Goddess grants wishes not merely for our whims and pleasure. I explained that often the granting of a wish could come with a life lesson, one that could be harsh. Brenna was willing to take the risk. She explained she often saw the young warrior at court in the Chieftain's council chambers discussing battles and ways to keep the village safe. If only he would notice her, she could charm her way into his heart. But, until now she had not found a way."

"And so, my dear, did you grant Brenna's request?"

"Well, Auntie, not at first because she was so secretive about which young man was her desire. She also was not willing to give me too much information about him. She was afraid somehow that, if she said too many things about him, her secret would be out and the young warrior would feel as if he had been tricked into finding favor with her. I explained that if I were to bring the Goddess a request, I must have enough details to make the wish a believable request," continued Caolyn.

"So, you received the information and you went to the Goddess with the request?"

"Yes," answered Caolyn, "I waited until the stars were shining and walked to the sacred well with the herbs needed for the wishing spell. I took with me Vervain to protect me, but also in hopes that with the wish made to Caolainn would be seen as pure and honest. I also took Yarrow, which is known to help the feelings of love, and a basil leaf on which I wrote 'Brenna's Warrior,' as she would not tell me his name. As I was blending the herbs, I was thinking of Ronan and how perhaps I should do a wishing spell for myself. I stopped to gather my thoughts and spoke the wishing spell."

Cynara was trying not to show any emotion, but in her heart, she knew that the inexperienced maiden was not doing things in the correct manner. Yes, she was right to protect herself with Vervain, to use Yarrow to induce human love and the basil leaf inscribed with the warrior's name. By her writing "Brenna's warrior," the spell could be granted with several warriors who desired Brenna to pursue her and might not even be the one of her heart's desire. Caolyn's voice came back to Cynara.

"By the power of three, Goddess of wishes grant for me
I ask not for my heart, but for my friend
Bring her a love that is pure and free
Bring her a love that is true and will not end
On this day bring this love I beg of thee."

"Then, Auntie, I looked toward the sky and saw a shooting star. I took it to be a sign from the Goddess, and I dropped the basil leaf and the herbs into the sacred well."

"And so, my dear Caolyn, what transpired?" The words were barely out of Cynara's mouth when Caolyn's eyes filled with tears.

"After I completed the spell, I went to Brenna and explained what I had done. She was very pleased, but she still would not tell me the warrior's name. So, after our visit I returned to the House of Maidens, and washed myself in the lake, and went to my chamber to sleep. The next day the Lady Ava sent one of the youngest maidens to me with a message to come to her. I quickly prepared myself and went to the Lady's door, waiting to be asked to enter. I was allowed into the room and stood before her. "

"My dear Caolyn," the Lady began, "there is a young warrior at the door asking my permission to see you. We cannot allow men to enter the house of Maidens unless they have been invited. I have asked him to meet you in the outer courtyard. Please advise him he is not to attempt to gain entrance unless invited. I will have to report him to his Chieftain if he does not comply."

"Auntie, I was so shocked to think a young man was asking for me. I did not know how to respond. I begged the Lady's pardon and asked to take my leave, which she granted but, I noticed a slight smile on her face. She looked at me and said, 'He seems quite smitten, my dear, go now. He has quite a pleasant countenance.'

"I could feel the warmth in my face and knew that it must be scarlet! I neared the outer courtyard; I knew before he turned to me that it was Ronan. My thoughts became scattered; my heart beat like the hooves of a hundred horses. Was Ronan Brenna's warrior? Was he here to ask about Brenna? He knows we are like sisters; perhaps he wants a few suggestions on how to win her heart. I straightened my skirts and walked toward him. When he turned, though, the look bestowed on me was one of desire. His smile was like sunshine. I could not stop gazing into his eyes as I floated towards him."

"'My lady,'" he said with a respectful nod of his head. 'I know we have not met properly, but I pray you will allow me to introduce myself. I am the warrior known as Ronan and I would like to know whose permission I must gain in order to court you?'

"Auntie, my heart stopped! This could not be happening! I wished his love to be showered on Brenna, not on me! And yet, my heart could not seem to stop jumping for joy that he wanted me. I was so confused.

I told him that I was pledged to my studies, but that I could find someone for him to ask for courting rights to my hand. I stammered and stuttered like a frightened child. I explained I had neither sire nor brother to ask for permission, but perhaps the Lady or you could grant this permission. He said he would be back to see me once he had been granted proper permission and then he took my hand and kissed it."

"I was now concerned that this could not be. I had just made the wish the night before and now Ronan was here. Did my thinking of him before I made the wish cause a mistake? Was Brenna also receiving a young warrior this morn? What if Brenna's warrior was also Ronan? How could this happen? I knew I had to seek out Brenna and see if she had any results from the wishing spell."

Through the entire last portion of the story Caolyn was crying softly. Cynara had the feeling the source of her sorrow was not fully disclosed as yet. While Caolyn had been unburdening her soul, Cynara had been thinking of all the mistakes that had been made with the wishing spell. What were the lessons the Goddess was trying to teach the young maiden by granting Caolyn's wish of the heart rather than her unselfish wish for her friend? Cynara knew that Vervain, did offer protection but often Yarrow in inexperienced hands could backfire. Also, Caolyn's poor judgement in thinking of Ronan as she prepared the herbs to drop in the sacred well could have caused a break in the spell. Once Cynara found out the rest of the story she and Caolyn together would find a way to ease the problem and, better yet, find a way to fix it entirely.

"So, Auntie, I quickly gathered myself together and called for a horse from the stables. Then, I rode as quickly as I could to Brenna. When I arrived at the Chieftain's camp, I went immediately to Brenna's guardian, her Aunt Arian. Arian advised me that I could see Brenna. She warned me that she was in a foul mood and even her most trusted servant could not seem to raise her spirits. I respectfully thanked the Lady Arian and went to Brenna's resting place."

"As I entered her room Brenna rose from her seat and dismissed her servant."

"You! What have you done?! I trusted you." Brenna was screaming at me.

"I to back away and sank to my knees."

By now, Caolyn was once again crying as she unburdened her heart. Cynara listened as the young maid went on.

"Brenna, I don't understand what happened! I came at once after I had a visit from Ronan. I.... Brenna cut me off."

"He came to visit you!" she screamed. "You must have wanted him for yourself all along. I trusted you and you tricked me!"

"No! No! I don't know what happened. I begged you for his name to do the spell, but you wouldn't give me his name. I sent the wish using 'Brenna's Warrior' for a name. Truly, Brenna, I would never betray you."

"That is not all that has happened," Brenna went on. "It seems that several warriors are asking my father to court me and I care not for any of them. Leave me, Caolyn, I am so angry! Fix this or trust me you shall pay and not only by the loss of our friendship!"

"I begged Brenna's forgiveness and left the room with a heavy heart. I kept thinking about the spell and what could have gone wrong. Auntie, can you help fix this?" Caolyn sobbed.

"My dear child," Cynara began. "I have several thoughts and questions about what may have gone wrong. But first, have you told me everything? It will do no good to have left out pieces of the story."

"Auntie, on the day that Ronan was at the House of Maidens, the Lady bid me to tell him he could not seek me out without her invitation. I was to go back to the Lady and report on the visit. I was so distraught that my only thought was Brenna. I did not report back to the Lady. I came to you instead and you saw the state I was in on my arrival."

"Well, my little maid, it seems that you have much to learn and fix with regards to this situation. I think we should start with the Lady Ava. She is of gentle nature and has much patience with young maidens in training. This being so, believe me when I say that you do not want to destroy her trust. It will be of no benefit to you to compromise your standing in the House. You still have much to learn, and I promised your mother I would see to your education and life lessons. I will not betray my promise to her. So, we will start with the Lady Ava."

III

Cynara and Caolyn prepared for their visit to the Lady Ava at the House of Maidens. "You must enter her chamber with humility and sorrow for having taken your leave without first reporting on your visit with Ronan, my dear," Cynara began. "And we must bring her an offering to help plead for her forgiveness. She will interpret your leave as being haughty and independent. Haughtiness is never a quality to be admired, especially in one who serves the Goddess and her Servant, the Lady of the House. I think the Lady Ava will forgive your independence. The House teaches independence, which is necessary to practice in service to the Goddess and others. Now, let me think, what we can bring as an appropriate gift to show your repentance?"

"Auntie, I am truly sorry and my humility will be seen by the Lady if she will allow us into her chambers. I don't know what makes me feel worse, my show of disrespect to the Lady or my bumbling of a wishing spell to help Brenna."

"If and when you see the Lady," Cynara began, "your feelings of repentance for being disrespectful had best be the strongest feeling. The Lady Ava will be able to tell if your heart is not truthful. As for Brenna, you will find a way to mend that friendship once I show you where your mistakes lay with regards to the wishing spell. The Goddess of Wishes is not one to whom I have often gone, but I do understand, as do all who serve the Goddess, the importance of carefully making a spell. My strength lies in the use of herbs and medicinal plants, and my knowledge is blessed by the Goddess herself. Come now, I have an idea what to bring the Lady Ava. Once we gather the things I need, we can begin our journey to the House of Maidens. It has been a while since I have visited, and perhaps my visit will also please the Lady."

Cynara and Caolyn spent the morning gathering herbs and plants to bring as gifts for the Lady Ava and the House. Cynara went to her garden and gathered lavender for relaxation, willow bark for pain and for a body when raging with fever. She also picked feverfew, which comforted wound, and bone injuries that could occur in battle, as well as head and toothaches. Lastly, she gathered blueberries and peppermint to make an enjoyable tea for cool nights. Peppermint, Cynara remembered, was one of Lady Ava's favorite teas.

Once inside her home, she set Caolyn to work packing the herbs and plants in small muslin sacks to keep them dry on the journey.

"Caolyn, once you have finished with the plants and herbs go to the trunk where you found the robe you have on now. There should be some other things of your mother's and of mine from my younger days. See what is appropriate and wear something suitable for the journey. I will go and pack my things and then we can be on our way."

"Yes, Auntie, I am nearly done. I will be quick. I only need to gather my soiled robes and pack them to bring back. If we leave soon, we should arrive at the House before the sun sets," Caolyn said as she finished stacking the sacks of herbs.

Preparing to leave, Caolyn harnessed her horse to the old cart Cynara used for her excursions into the forest to gather plants. Cynara's old mule brayed softly as Caolyn was working. "I am sorry, old Dob," Caolyn said to the animal. "You can barely take Cynara around now that you are old. My horse is faster, and we must make good time on our journey. We will let you roam free in the gated pasture, and you will have plenty to eat and drink. Cynara will return soon. You'll see." Caolyn spoke gently while scratching the faithful Dob on his neck. Dob returned the remarks with another soft bray. Caolyn led both animals out of the barn and steered Dob to the pasture, locking the gate.

"The cart is ready, Auntie," Caolyn called. Cynara soon had her bundles placed in the cart. She also had a basket filled with food and drink for their journey. Her intent was to stop and have a light meal on route. She also hoped that she might talk to Caolyn about what had gone wrong with the spell and prepare her for what the Lady might expect on her arrival.

"A moment, Caolyn. I have a treat for Dob before I go, and I must guard my door with a protection spell. Then we can be off." Cynara walked to the old mule and held out a sweet carrot from the garden. "Here, my friend. I will be back soon," Cynara gently brushed the old mule's head with her hand. She then walked to the door of her cottage and said.

"Three times the rings go round
Keeping all that is evil on the ground
Should evil dare to come to this place
It is barred from my sacred space
The rings go round three times three
My space is protected, let it be"

Cynara walked three circles around the cottage, moving the sacred energy of the spell into place as she spoke. Once the spell was completed, she turned, and smiled at Caolyn, and said, "We are off, my child. "The journey has begun."

IV

The mid-summer day was beautiful to behold. The sun was shining, the sky was blue, and a gentle breeze cooled the two women.

"You are doing quite well with the horse and cart, Caolyn. I know all maidens at the House are expected to learn to ride the horses, but I was unaware that they are taught to manage a cart as well."

"Auntie, that should not be a surprise to you! You have managed a cart and mule for as long as I have known you. You know the maidens are taught to be self-sufficient women," Caolyn replied.

"Yes, my dear, that is true, but in my time at the House we learned only to ride a horse or mule. If a cart was needed, a man from the village would be called to assist us. I learned to manage a cart when I moved to the edge of the Great Woods. It became necessary if I wanted to travel about and find herbs and plants different from what I could grow or find near my home. I taught myself to use the cart once a farmer gave Dob to me. The farmer was getting old and no longer needed as many animals. Dob is more of a pet now than a work animal, but we both manage together." Cynara smiled as she spoke of her life and of how pleased she was to be spending time with Caolyn.

The time on the journey passed in happy conversation. Cynara listened as Caolyn spoke of her days at the House. She explained to Cynara that she had not yet decided on a specific area of practice in which to honor the Goddess.

The sun was rose higher in the sky as midday approached. "Are you ready to take lunch and rest a bit, Auntie?" Caolyn asked.

"Yes, we should stop, my dear. My old bones are uncomfortable with all of the rocking and bumping of the wagon. A break from the ride would be good. I have packed us some bread and berry jam. I have two wine skins, one with water and mashed blueberries and one with willow bark tea for my weary bones. Let's stop up ahead by the big oak tree. The shade will also be welcome."

Caolyn guided the wagon under the tree and went to the cart to gather their things for lunch. "Auntie, I think I can hear a brook or stream running. I will take the bucket from the wagon and fetching some water for the horse. Will you be all right while I go? Do you need my help for anything?"

"No, my dear, go on, I will prepare our meal." Cynara took the basket. As she started toward the tree to spread out their meal, the sky grew darker and the wind grew stronger.

"Be on guard!" Cynara heard as plain as day. She felt a sudden chill. The wind died away as quickly as it came, the wind died away and the sky was bright again. Cynara could not understand the feeling of uneasiness that overcame her. She suddenly thought of Caolyn alone at the stream. Walking as fast as she could she called

"Caolyn, Caolyn, answer me now!" She listened but heard only the stream babbling away. "Caolyn, Caolyn, where are you!" She was doing her best not to sound frantic.

"Auntie, I am right here!" Caolyn responded. "What is wrong? Are you ill?"

Cynara stopped and turned, her hand was on her heart. "I am better now that I see you! Did you not see the sky darken and the wind come up? I was afraid it would be raining and wanted you closer to the cart. I think I just need to have some food and tea."

Caolyn looked at her "auntie." She felt puzzled by Cynara's statement. "I did not see the sky darken, nor hear the wind, Auntie. Was it a vision?"

"No, no, my dear, sometimes I think my aging mind imagines things. Do not fret. Let us take our meal and be on our way. We do not want to be on these old paths at night." Cynara moved to the tree and sat down heavily. Caolyn joined her and they had their simple meal in peace, but she could not shake off the uneasiness that she felt. She knew she must stay alert. Something was afoot. She smiled at Caolyn, but, she could see the look of concern on the maiden's face. She did not want to have her worry unnecessarily about her. "I am fine, my dear. Do not be concerned. Enjoy your meal," Cynara smiled at Caolyn.

Caolyn smiled back, but she knew her "auntie" well enough to know that what was concerning her had nothing to do with her "old age." She hoped Cynara wasn't ill. She offered a silent prayer for protection to the Goddess as they finished their meal and prepared to be on their way again.

V

The early afternoon sun and warm air of the late summer day made for an enjoyable ride as the two women continued on their journey to the House of Maidens.

"We should arrive on time for the evening meal and salutation to the Goddess, Auntie," Caolyn began. She looked at Cynara and found her with her head drooping and bobbing. "Auntie, are you weary?"

Cynara jumped, a bit startled by the intrusion into her dozing in the warm sun. "I am, child," she began. "How much longer might we be traveling?"

We probably have about two hours before we see the village, and the House is probably a quarter hour or so outside the village to the north." Caolyn answered. "You have time enough for a short rest in the back of the wagon, if you'd like."

"Perhaps I will, my dear. Stop the cart for a moment and I will climb in the back and take my rest. I have not traveled to the House for some time, and it seems longer than I remember."

When the wagon halted, Cynara climbed into the back and lay down on the sheepskin rug on the wagon floor. "Are you settled, Auntie?" Caolyn asked. The only response was a muffled "hmmm." Caolyn smiled and started the wagon moving again. With Cynara at rest, she could prod the horse to go a little faster and not be so cautious in avoiding the bumps. This would speed their time to the village and House.

In the back of the wagon, Cynara was deeply asleep though it was not the restful sleep she hoped. She was dreaming of Caolyn and the wishing spell gone wrong. In her dreams she was making a list of what must be set right. How should the Lady Ava be approached? Should she seek audience first and plead Caolyn's case or let the young maiden take the brunt of anger head on? How could the relationship between Caolyn and Brenna be mended? She was not only a friend, but the Chieftain's daughter. Caution must be taken in order for the Chieftain not to be forced into a position of defending his daughter's hurt feelings, or Caolyn could be barred from village events and feasts. And then, there was the young warrior Ronan? Caolyn seemed smitten. How might that be fixed causing little or no harm to any of the young people? Cynara tossed and turned in the back of the wagon as it rolled on.

In Cynara's restless sleep, she now saw the sky turn black and the wind moving dark clouds. The voice again, "Be on guard!" Whose voice was it? It had a familiar tone and pitch to it, and yet, it was unrecognizable. It kept repeating the same phrase over and over as Cynara tossed and turned.

"FOR WHAT!!!" Cynara bolted awake screaming.

"What is wrong Auntie? You were screaming in your sleep! Are you ill? What troubles you, and do not tell me it is your age again. I am concerned for you, Auntie. Please tell me."

"My dear, I do not know what to tell you, but when

we were at midday meal I had a feeling of uneasiness come over me. It felt like a warning of something to come. And now, while trying to rest, I was dreaming of all you have said and I was trying to figure a way to solve the mistakes of the wishing spell. Then in my dream, the sky grew black, the wind came up, and the voice from the wind said to 'be on guard!' I do not yet understand what to be 'on guard' about. The voice was familiar in a way, but I could not determine who it could be. I will have to be attentive to all the signs that may come our way on this journey. Rest assured, you and I will find a resolution to this dilemma while we mend the fences broken by the wishing spell."

"Auntie, I am filled with sorrow knowing now that I have dragged you into my mistakes. I sought your counsel because I did not know where else to go. I knew you could be trusted to have my best interest at heart. Forgive me," Caolyn cried as she spoke.

"Caolyn, I am here for you always as I promised your mother. Do not be full of worry over this; all things will come to pass in the Goddess' own time. We will be attentive to her signs and be watchful for her guidance. Perhaps the voice to 'be on guard' is her own. We shall see." Cynara leaned over to pat Caolyn's back. "Now, we must be close to the village; I can see smoke in the distance. It is probably coming from hearth fires. I will sit back here and organize our gifts while you continue with the cart. Stop just before the village gate, and I will freshen my face with some water and straighten my robes before entering the village. Be at peace my child. This too will pass."

"As you wish, Auntie," Caolyn responded. But, in her heart and head she felt troubled by the thought of having caused any difficulties for her beloved auntie.

Just as requested, Caolyn stopped the wagon just outside the village. The two women stepped out of the wagon, shook off some of the dust from the road, and washed their faces and hands with water from the wine skin. Once refreshed, they climbed back in and proceeded to the village gate.

"Ho, Stad!" the guard called from the gate.

Caolyn stood up. "It is I, Caolyn, from the House of Maidens with my aunt. We wish passage through the village as we travel on to the House."

"Caolyn, come, you may enter," the guard replied. As Caolyn approached, she recognized the young warrior as Aedan, one of Ronan's companions. "You have been long away, Caolyn. I fear you have caused Ronan some worry," he said with a teasing smile.

"I have been spending some time with my Auntie, the wise woman Cynara. She is a healer from the Great Woods." Caolyn could feel the heat rising in her cheeks as she spoke. "I am sure Ronan has much to occupy his mind without worrying about my whereabouts."

Aedan smiled as he opened the gate and nodded his head, "As you say, Caolyn. Come, enter the village. May I have your permission to tell Ronan I have seen your return?"

"Young man," Cynara interrupted. "Do not tease her so. It is of no consequence if you tell your friend or not. We do not have time to dally; we must be at the House of Maidens for evening repast and prayer. Please allow us to make haste."

"Of course," Aedan said still grinning. "I have been long at the gate and seek a little diversion from the boring day."

As Caolyn guided the wagon through the gate,

Cynara noticed him wink at Caolyn. This even made her smile as she thought how nice it was to be young.

Passing through the village went loner than she had hoped. Men were returning from the fields. Shopkeepers were closing their tents and settling things for the night ahead. One could smell the hearth fires and the cooking evening meals. Cynara was remembering what it had been like to be raised in this village. People were always about, someone to talk with about the day and how it had been spent. She was lost in remembering when she heard someone call her name.

"CYNARA, is it you!" The voice was male and not really recognizable, but familiar. She turned toward the voice as Caolyn brought the wagon to a halt.

"Who is it? State your name." Cynara began. She looked at the male figure. He was unkempt, with overly long hair and a heavy beard.

The man started to laugh. "Surely, it has not been so long for you to not recognize the brother of your dearest friend, your sister maiden!"

"DREST, can it be you? I believed you long dead!" Cynara exclaimed. "Caolyn, help me down from the wagon, now!"

Caolyn assisted her auntie down but she was totally confused. "Who was this man, and where had she heard this name before?" she wondered. She watched as the two apparent old friends embraced each other.

"The years have been kind to you, Cynara," the man spoke. "Not so for me."

"Drest, you have let your spirit be overcome with self-pity. You do not care for your body in even the most basic of ways. We all have our sufferings, but when one has life, it must be honored. Life is a blessing from the gods." Cynara spoke as she stepped back from the worn old man.

"Cynara, when I could not avenge my sister as was her wish, and my wounds from the battle that killed her healed, my spirit was broken beyond belief. I left the village and sought comfort in the highlands. The mist and fog covered my body as grief covered my soul. Now I am old and have come home to spend my days with my kinsmen."

Caolyn was taking in the conversation and suddenly it came! This was her uncle, her mother's only brother! Even she had been told he had wandered away and died from a broken spirit. "Uncle!" she exclaimed as she hurried toward him. "Uncle, you are alive!"

Drest looked at the beautiful young maiden coming toward him. His face drained of color and Cynara moved, to keep him upright. Caolyn caught him as he stumbled, but she did not let him fall. "Gods, you are the picture of Myra!" he exclaimed. And then he collapsed.

"Caolyn, the wineskin with water, fetch it, quickly!" Cynara yelled. She turned toward Drest and pleaded. "Do not leave me old friend, you whom I believed to be long dead! Goddess hear my prayer. Do not take him from us!"

Caolyn quickly brought the wineskin filled with water and placed it to her uncle's lips. He started to sip and swallow. Caolyn also poured some water over his face and wiped it with a soft muslin cloth. Slowly Drest began to come around. When he opened his eyes, he smiled, "Myra, I have finally seen you again. I have come to you at last in the other world."

Caolyn was taken aback by her uncle's words. "Uncle, it is I, Caolyn, Myra's daughter. Thank the gods you are still among us!"

Drest became more and more aware of his surroundings and slowly sat up. "Child, how blessed I am to have found you. I knew your mother had left you in Cynara's care at the House of Maidens, but I have only recently returned to the village. I have not had the courage to go to the House to see if you might still be there. I could not take another sadness."

Cynara interrupted the discussion. "We are going on to the House of Maidens this night. Drest, you cannot go to the house in such a state. Where are you staying? You must freshen and clean yourself or the Lady will not allow you entrance."

"I have been staying in my old home at the north side of the village. It was abandoned and is in disrepair, but it provides shelter."

Cynara went to the wagon. She fumbled about, searching for a few things. She found a bit of cloth and carefully placed the mark of her role as a healer on the cloth. The mark was a cup with herbs on the base and flames in the cup. She walked back to Drest. "Here, show my mark to the Chieftain," she began. Tell him you were one of the village warriors in years past. Tell him your name. Your father, now, passed, also served as a warrior. Tell him you are my friend. He will give you shelter, a warm bath and fresh clothes. Warriors of days past are always respected and given shelter for their service. Explain to him you seek audience with the Lady Ava to inquire about your sister's child. He will understand and want to hear more of your story." She also handed him some lavender and mint. "Add these to your bath and scrub well. Make yourself well again in body and your spirit will follow. I will see you soon at the House of Maidens. Come, Caolyn, we must finish our journey."

"But, Auntie, should we not bring Uncle to the Chieftain?" Caolyn questioned.

Cynara turned, but before she could speak, Drest began, "Go, my child. My heart is lighter having seen you and my old friend. Cynara is right. I must take charge of my own spirit. I will see you soon and I will be much improved. I promise."

VI

Caolyn and Cynara climbed back on the wagon and continued on to the House of Maidens. After watching them go, Drest turned and headed toward the Chieftain's compound at the south side of the village. "Finally, a bit of good fortune," he thought.

Once outside the village gate, Caolyn began speaking to Cynara. "Auntie, how can it be that my mother's brother is alive? I believed him to be long removed from this world"

"I cannot answer what I do not know to be truth," Cynara began. "When your mother passed to the other world, your uncle Drest became a broken man. He felt that she was taken because he never sought revenge for her. The man who sired you was taken by another woman in another village. Myra, your mother, was not aware of this when the feasting of Beltane was taking place. They were only two young spirits overcome by the feast and celebration of spring. This is why, Caolyn, we must be careful of things which involve the heart. Your wishing spell gone wrong has now set a multiple of hearts, including your own, in turmoil. We must set this right."

"But, Auntie, you are not explaining how it came

to be that everyone believed uncle to be dead!" Caolyn responded.

"The way I understand the story," Cynara continued, "is that after your uncle discovered who your sire was, he went to his village, to confront him and ask that he do the right thing. When Drest discovered that he was not only pledged to another but had two young ones, and the woman was carrying another, he took caution not to cause disharmony within the family circle. When Drest returned to your mother, he vowed to her he would go back and bring revenge and justice for her. Your mother was strong in her wishes not to destroy the warrior's family. Instead, she told Drest that she would foster out the babe if it was a son and she would raise a girl with her in the House of Maidens. Your uncle honored her wishes and seemed content with the decision, but then when the village and House were attacked by a band of Gauls, your mother was mortally wounded. Drest fought in the battle and was wounded himself. When he heard of the loss of his sister a few days after the battle, he could not be consoled. He was cared for at the House, and though his wounds were not healed, he set out on a quest to seek revenge for his sister and you. It was assumed when he did not return to the village that somewhere on his quest he left this world for the next. No one had seen him since."

Caolyn listened to the story with misty eyes. Silence settled between the two women. Cynara was at a loss for words of comfort because she still could not believe that Drest was alive. As for Caolyn, her thoughts were saddened by her lack of blood family and being somewhat pleased that her only blood relative, believed dead, was now alive. She silently prayed to the Goddess that he be granted more time on this earth, so she could get to speak with him and learn more about her family.

"Look, Caolyn," began Cynara. "I can see the tall spire of the house. The sun is setting on it and it looks as beautiful as I remember. We will soon be there. It has been an interesting journey, my dear, has it not?"

Caolyn looked up at the sunset and the spire and felt a conflicting sense of peace and anxiety. Peace to be home and anxiety over what now lay ahead in fixing all that had changed since she left. "Yes, Auntie, it has been interesting, and I believe that it will continue to be interesting for a while. I am glad to be home though."

The two women arrived at the gate of the house and Caolyn stepped down to unlock the gate.

"By the power of three, Goddess, I ask of thee
Unlock this gate and set it free
Go to my home, I return to thee
This I ask so mote it be "

The gate swung open and Caolyn and Cynara passed easily through. Caolyn stood in the wagon and turned back to the gate. A wave of her hand and the gate closed behind them. A feeling of peace settled over the two women as they went forward to the House.

As Caolyn pulled the wagon to a halt, she heaved a sigh and looked at Cynara. "What a journey you and I have had, Auntie. "I went to you heavy hearted and shared my burden. Your consenting to help me which greatly relieved my distress. Yet, I am feeling a little guilty having brought you into all of this. But now, to see now to see my uncle Drest, alive…."

"We never know what life may give us, but surely it has been an interesting time for both of us," Cynara agreed. "We will have little time to think upon any of this now. We must prepare ourselves to meet the Lady Ava. May the Goddess guide us through the meeting."

As Cynara was speaking, a young stable boy appeared and bowed to the women. "Caolyn, you are back. You have been missed."

"Thank you Brian," Caolyn said sweetly to the young boy. "I have missed you too. Will you come around and help my Auntie down from the wagon? We must make haste to clean ourselves before we seek audience with the Lady Ava," Caolyn said as she stepped down from the wagon and ruffled the boy's hair.

"Auntie, this is Brian. He has been fostered to us by his widowed mother, and he is the best stable boy we have. He also is quick witted and loves to learn all manner of things. I have been teaching him how to dry and preserve herbs from the garden."

"Hello, Brian," Cynara replied. "If you are wanting for knowledge of plants, I can be of great help to you in the time we have here."

"Thank you, Mam. If I finish my duties early, may I seek you out?"

"I would be most pleased if you did, son. I have much I can teach you."

"Imagine, a young boy interested in the way of the plants," she thought. "Perhaps we have a young Druid, healer in our midst."

"Caolyn," Brian began. "I have heard much talk among the maidens. Lady Ava was at first angry when you took your leave without telling her. Once you were gone and not found she was gravely concerned for your safety. Also, Ronan has been wandering about like a love-sick puppy," Brian said with a smile.

"Now, young Sir, how many times have I had to warn you about snooping!" Caolyn said while shaking her finger at the boy.

"Aw, Caolyn, how can I learn the happenings at the House if I don't snoop?" Brian said with a chuckle.

"You'd best be careful my, boyo. You do not want to lose your position here, nor do you want to be on Lady Ava's bad side."

"Enough, you two," Cynara interrupted. "We must make haste if we are to see the Lady this night. The sooner you ask forgiveness, Caolyn, the sooner we can be about the business of setting things right again. We also have Drest to consider. We must find a way to help him be strong again. Come!"

Caolyn tousled Brian's hair again and promised to see him before the night was through. She and Cynara went through the large archway into the inner courtyard of the House. "Now it begins," she thought. "Help me, Goddess, to mend what I have broken. Protect and be with me during this trial."

VII

Cynara was lost in her own thoughts. They were first of Caolyn and fixing the wishing spell gone wrong. Then the thoughts turned toward the warning voices she had heard and finally to her old friend Drest. Surely as the sun rose in the day there were signs she must be on the watch for and be ready to help Caolyn if needed.

Caolyn and Cynara went through the doors of the House and onto the stone path to the Chamber of Waters. The chamber was really a walled garden that could be entered only from the House. Inside the chamber, a huge stone pool had been dug and formed for the women in the House to bathe. Water was brought in daily from the lake in barrels, then heated on fires and poured into the pool. When the ladies had finished their ministrations, a small portion of wall was hoisted up on pulleys, and the dirty water flowed back out and helped to water the grounds around the house.

Once they were inside the chamber, a maiden about of about twelve years came to the women and asked if they would like to bathe. Cynara turned and responded to the maiden. "Yes, wee one, we would enjoy a chance to refresh ourselves. What is your name?"

"My name is Nora and I have been here at the house

41

only a few days, but I am very good at drawing the water for cleansing," she said with a smile.

Caolyn asked the young girl if she would need assistance in tipping the heated water into the pool. "No, lady, I can do it. I came from my father's farm and I am quite strong for my age. I am so happy to be at the House and learning new things. Will you be needing any garments in addition to the water?"

"No dear, we have brought our own clean garments and they will suit us well. We need to make haste because we will be wanting to seek audience with the Lady Ava before evening gathering. Do you think we can do that?" Caolyn asked.

"I know that you want to see her and I have told the Lady Ava that you have arrived."

Caolyn and Cynara looked at each other a little surprised. "But how, could you…?" Caolyn began.

Cynara interrupted and looked at the girl, "I can see that you have a gift, young Nora. You have a bit of the gift of fey, am I right?"

"Yes, Lady," Nora responded. "My mam brought me to Lady Ava because she said I was always telling her of things to come. She told Lady Ava I frightened her. She feared there was something wrong with me. Lady Ava assured my mam that there was nothing wrong but that the Goddess had granted me a gift. Lady Ava said the House of Maidens would be a good place to learn more about my gift, if my mam would let me stay. There are seven others to feed at home, so here I am," Nora responded.

"Well, you are in a good place to learn many things," Cynara began. "Can you tell us if the Lady's anger has been raised with our arrival?"

"That, I cannot say, Lady. I can say that she was most

joyful when she first heard that you were about to arrive."

"You are wise beyond your years, little one. Never tell anyone things about the Lady Ava without her permission," Cynara responded. "Now let us refresh ourselves, and you can advise the Lady that we are ready to see her when she is ready to receive us."

Nora went quickly to the heated water barrels and pulled the great rope that tilted the water into the pool. Cynara and Caolyn were soon in the pool. Nora came running over with lavender and mint to perfume the water and to rub it into their hair and skin. Soon the women were out of the bath and dressed.

Nora asked Caolyn. "My Lady, would you like me to braid your hair with yellow daisies? I know you like them."

Caolyn was going to how she could that but stopped herself. "You do have a gift, Nora. Yes, please braid my hair, but call me Caolyn, as all of my sisters in the house do." Nora smiled and began to braid Caolyn's hair.

Once they were ready, Caolyn took Cynara to the table room where the maidens and members of the House took their meals. "It is long past the evening meal, Auntie, but we can at least have tea and bread."

"That is more than enough, Caolyn," Cynara began. "I am a bundle of nerves at this moment. Remember to be submissive and implore the Lady's forgiveness. This is a time to be thankful that your mother and Lady Ava were maidens together. She has fond memories of Myra as do I. She also has a tender spot for those who have been left motherless."

"I will be most humble, Auntie. I have practiced in my mind what I must say, and I have prayed to the Goddess for guidance."

No sooner had Caolyn spoken the words when one of Lady Ava's maid servants entered and announced that the Lady Ava was ready to receive them.

Cynara followed the young maiden with Caolyn walking behind. They went through a dimly lit passageway into what was known in the House as the Gathering Hall. At one end of the hall was a slightly raised platform with a beautiful, carved oak chair. The chair had symbols for several goddesses carved into various places. The wood at the back of the chair had a carving of the symbol representing the Triple Goddess. The symbol was the waxing, full and waning moon all joined together. The waxing moon represented the young maidens not yet at the peak of their womanhood. The full moon represented the mother or time of a woman's fertility and child bearing. The waning moon represented the crone or wise woman who had by her life experiences reached a time of wisdom and understanding of life. The Lady Ava was not yet present in the Hall. The young maiden bade the two women to be seated, and she quietly left them.

Whispering, Cynara spoke to Caolyn. "Perhaps the Lady's absence is a good sign. If she were greatly angered, I fear she would be waiting to dole out punishment or reprimand for your absence. Take heart, dear, this will soon be behind us."

As Cynara spoke, the women could hear the Lady Ava enter the room. Cynara and Caolyn stood up and bowed their heads as a sign of respect to the Lady. Lady Ava sat in the carved oak chair and spoke. "Raise your heads, my daughters. Cynara, you have been long gone from us; it is good to see you again."

"Thank you, my Lady. I did not realize how much I

have missed the House until I saw it once again. I have chosen the solitary life as you know, and the habit is hard to break," Cynara spoke in a soft and respectful tone.

"Yes, as we get on in years, we like to stay with the things that are comfortable to us." It was not missed that during the conversation, the Lady Ava did not even glance at Caolyn, who was beginning to feel faint with anxiety. Soon the pleasantries were stopped, and Lady Ava bid Cynara to be seated.

"Now, my young maid, Caolyn, have you had time to think on the disrespect that you have shown me and this House?"

Caolyn looked up. Her heart was pounding so hard she feared the drumming must be heard by those in the room. She looked up at Lady Ava and began to speak. "I have come to ask your forgiveness. I know I was wrong leaving in haste, but I was trying to make a wish for a friend and....."

"Stop, Caolyn!" Lady Ava began, standing and raising her hand. "This House and the path you have chosen to follow must never be taken for granted. You have pledged yourself to us and the Goddess. You must always put that first. On the day that you left the House in such haste, were you not granted my permission to see the young warrior who had sought you out? Were you not told to report back to me once you had advised him that he could not seek you here without having a proper introduction?" Lady Ava paused and looked sternly at the young woman before her. "Well, have you nothing to say, Child?"

Cynara began to stand up. "My Lady, if ....." Lady Ava raised her hand to Cynara.

"You and I will discuss Caolyn's behavior later,

Cynara. For now, let her explain herself." Cynara sat down feeling helpless. She was unable to come to Caolyn's aid but the young woman, must be able to express herself. She must also be able to defend herself if she were to continue in the House.

"My Lady," Caolyn began. "My friend Brenna had asked me to make a wishing spell for a young warrior that she wished to have court her. She would not tell me his name, so I wrote the words 'Brenna's Warrior' on the basil leaf before I dropped it into the wishing well. On the day that Ronan showed himself at the House, I was taken by surprise. I had met him at Beltane and desired to see him again. When I went to greet him and explain your instructions, he apologized. He then asked whose permission he must seek to court me. He promised me that he would return when he had found a proper way to court me. Once he took his leave, I feared something had gone wrong with my spell. Without thinking, I ran to Brenna to see if anything had happened to her. When I explained that Ronan had come to the House she became enraged and said I had tricked her." The tears could not be held back any longer. Through tears and sobs Caolyn finished the story. She told Lady Ava that now several warriors were seeking Brenna and she wanted none, only Ronan. She ended her story with her arrival at Cynara's home.

Lady Ava sat and listened to the tale of wishes gone wrong and of young love and friendship in shambles. In her mind, she was angry with the show of disrespect, but in her heart, she felt sympathy for these young maidens who were attempting to follow the age-old path of the Goddess. The House was there to mold them in the way of the Goddess, to have respect for all life, and to think independently and with strength. Caolyn was certainly displaying independence and strength when she took it upon herself to go to her friend in need without asking permission. But still, there would have to be some discipline dispensed to the maiden. Lady Ava stood up.

Caolyn had been sitting for what seemed to be an endless time of quiet. She could hear Cynara breathing, but she could not bear to look over at her to get a sense of what she thought. As for Cynara, she too was uneasy with the stillness of the room and what seemed to be an extreme length of time before Lady Ava stood.

"Rise my daughter," Lady Ava began. Caolyn rose from her seat and stood with her head bent in humility. Lady Ava came down from the raised platform and went to her. She placed her hands on her shoulders and bid Caolyn to look up. When Caolyn faced the Lady, she did not see anger in her eyes, rather she saw compassion and understanding.

"Caolyn, you have disappointed me and disrespected my authority over you by taking a sudden leave. You know that maidens such as yourself mean a lot to me. Those of you without mothers become like my own children because I have never borne a child ,but I have always desired one. You are especially dear because your mother was also one of us. I cannot let you escape some punishment for your folly. I am responsible for all of you that reside in the House. It was disrespectful to leave in the manner that you did, but then to be gone for days with no word of where you were! I feared for your welfare!"

Lady Ava looked toward Cynara, who stood facing the Lady's gaze. "Cynara, thank the Goddess she was with you. This was my hope and prayer." Lady Ava turned back to Caolyn. "My daughter, first you will assist little Nora for days times three. This is so you will gain back a sense of humility in caring for others and their needs. After three days pass, you will send word to the young warrior who seeks your company. You will remind him to seek proper ways to court you, if that is what he desires. Cynara is here now and he can consult with her for permission. Lady Ava turned toward Cynara who nodded her head in agreement.

"Now, as for all of this mess with wishes gone wrong and Brenna being besieged by warriors she does not want, this I leave to you and Cynara to fix. Cynara's wisdom will be of great help to you. You best take heed and be sure that your wishing spells do no harm. I can't be having this confusion of feelings around the House. This is a place for seeking the path not for matchmaking. Do you understand?"

"Yes, Lady, I am also most grateful for your kindness in dealing with my mistakes," Cynara said with her head bowed in respect.

"Now Cynara, let you and I take leave and go to my chambers for a bit of nourishment. I also hope that our conversation will be good for our spirits as we have not seen each other for way too long." Lady Ava walked to Cynara and gave her old friend a hug of welcome.

Lady Ava turned toward Caolyn and spoke. "Take a bit of time with Nora. She can explain your duties for the next three days. I trust that she already knows you are coming. Her gift of things to be grows stronger each day."

"Yes, Lady, and again thank you for your words," Caolyn said as she bowed her head and turned to leave the Gathering Hall. Her heart was less heavy now. She knew that she had been given a light punishment. She smiled thinking of spending three days with the sweet young

Nora. She also wondered what Nora might be seeing in the days to come. As she walked from the hall, she could hear her auntie and Lady Ava talking and laughing as if they were young maidens again. It was good to have her auntie the back in the House.

VIII

Walking toward the sleeping chambers, Caolyn hoped to find young Nora preparing for the evening gathering, which began at the rising of the moon. This was the month of the Green Plant or Wyrt Moon. The moon was in the waning phase. It was believed to be the time to banish negativity in all that surrounds the world. "This is a good time to pray to the Goddess to banish any negative feeling Brenna may still hold against me," Caolyn thought as she walked toward the sleeping chambers of the youngest girls.

"Caolyn, my elder sister, I believe you are looking for me," Nora's voice surprised Caolyn.

"You must not startle me so, Nora," Caolyn began. "We are to begin working with each other on the morrow. I have come for instructions."

"The instructions are simple." Nora began. "You are to be with me for three days. I can't understand why the Lady thought you should be with me. These duties are far below your status."

"As you know, I have disrespected the Lady and the House. My punishment is to teach me more humility by caring for others while I assist you, Nora. I hope that Lady Ava also felt I could learn more about your gift of fey, while we are together," Caolyn finished.

"I don't know what I can teach you about my gift. It just happens. It is like a thought or a dream passing through my eyes. Often things make no sense, but the Lady assures me that, in time, I will come to learn the meanings of many signs, and those things can be of help to the House, the village and our people," Nora stated.

"Nora, one thing I have learned," Caolyn began, "is that all things happen in their proper time. We cannot hurry things along. The Goddess knows the right timing for all things upon the earth. She doles her blessings and punishments as she sees fit. Come, we have a little time for the instructions I will need for tomorrow. We can go back to the Chamber of Waters, and once you have explained my duties, we can go out to the prayer circle through the back of the chamber. We do not want to be late for the evening blessings."

They walked toward the Chamber of Waters. The path was dimly lit by torches and the two were making their way along when Nora grabbed Caolyn's hand and held it tightly. Caolyn could feel the girl trembling.

"What is it, Nora? Are you fearful?" Caolyn asked.

"Sister, stop, I fear there is something sad that will be in your future. I can't determine what it is at this time, but a voice has told me to '*be on guard.*'

"Nora, there is no reason to be fearful in the House. Each night a protection spell is chanted and there are always two warriors on guard to warn of any intrusion," Caolyn advised.

"No, Caolyn, I am not fearful for our persons. I am fearful that you are going to experience a sadness of the heart."

Caolyn comforted Nora with a hug and told her not

to worry. "Things of the heart are often difficult, but we manage to survive. Do not be so fearful for my heart."

As Caolyn spoke to Nora, she was remembering the trip to the house with Cynara. She remembered Cynara saying that she too heard a voice with the same message. This was strange. Nora and Cynara had no connection. How could they be hearing the same message and was it from the same voice? Caolyn was jostled from her thinking by Nora's voice.

"Caolyn, you are not listening! We have to hurry or we will be late for evening blessing. Look, the water is heated with the fires. Brian will come and light the fires and then we must watch for the steam to rise. Then we wait for the members of the House who desire bathing to come. I will help you with tipping the barrels. It is not difficult, but at first you must learn to balance properly so you do not get wet." Nora started to laugh, "When I first began assisting in the Chamber, I had to change my clothes many times. I was as wet as the bathers."

Caolyn laughed and said, "Ah yes, but I will have you for help, so I should be spared. Come, let's be off to prayer. We can worry about the other instructions tomorrow."

The two girls started out through the chamber door that led to the prayer circle in the garden. The waning Wryt moon was beginning to rise. Women of the House, young and old, gathered around the large circle drawn in the garden. In the center of the circle were three lighted, white candles. Each candle was representative of the three symbols of the Goddess. Lady Ava stepped into the center of the circle draped in a white cloak. She circled the candles three times and stopped. Instructing the women to clasp hands, she bowed her head in prayer.

Everyone followed her movement. After a short time, she raised her hands and prayed.

> "Goddess at the end of this day, bless us now as we pray.
> The waning of the green plant moon take with you our woe and gloom.
> Negative feelings of jealousy and hate take with you,
> Leave happiness in your wake.
> Replace all negative feelings with harmony and love
> Let us see you in the symbol of the white dove
> Blessings upon this house we beseech of
> This we ask, so mote it be."

The women raised their heads at the end of the prayer. Lady Ava spread lavender over the flames and the beautiful calming scent spread over the group as they quietly walked to their sleeping chambers.

IX

Caolyn finally felt calm and still. The evening prayer circle always had a way of making the anxieties of the day or of life start to recede from one's spirit. She had prayed that the Goddess would remove all negativity from her relationship with Brenna. She was a good friend, but being the Chieftain's daughter, she was also used to having everything her way. She would probably be a great leader or the wife of a great leader someday, but time would tell.

The other thought swirling around in Caolyn's mind was of Ronan. Now that she was aware that it was Ronan that Brenna wanted, what was to become of her own feelings for him? She walked on to the chamber deep in thought.

As Caolyn passed by a window she heared her name being called. "Caolyn, Caolyn, if you are there speak," the voice said.

The voice was familiar, but so faint she could not determine who it could be. She walked to the window and had to stand on tip toes to peer out. "Who is calling? It is time for the House to be at rest."

Out of the bushes came Brian, the stable boy. "Tis I, Brian, Caolyn. I thought you would come to see me before the night was over, as you promised. I have been worried about your fate and punishment by the Lady."

"Brian, I did not forget about you. The night has escaped me and there was no time left to seek you. I will see you on the morn. Lady Ava was most kind in dealing with my faults. I have been given the task of assisting Nora in the Chamber of Waters."

"So, you have met Nora? Is she not pleasant of face and spirit?" Brian asked. "You most definitely will see me, Caolyn. I have the duty of lighting the fires for the waters used in the bathing pool."

"She is most pleasant, Master Brian and intelligent. I see you have a special friend in her already," Caolyn teased.

"Aw, Caolyn, I just enjoy her company."

"Be careful, young sir, the Goddess Branwen can turn a young heart soft as butter if she chooses. Now be off before we both bring trouble on our heads. I will see you and Nora in the morn," Caolyn laughingly taunted as she rushed to her chamber.

X

In another part of the House, Lady Ava and Cynara were enjoying each other's company. They spent time sharing with each other all that had happened since the two were last together.

"So, Cynara," Lady Ava began, "You surely must have been taken by surprise to find Caolyn at your door. She is a high-spirited maiden, but she is also a devoted student. She is young and still untrained in the craft. She does not yet understand that the Goddess she was named for often uses wishes to teach lessons. These lessons can often be difficult, even cruel. She needs to understand how to protect herself when imploring the Goddess to grant a wish. Look what has come to be because of her inexperience."

"Yes, Lady," Cynara responded. "She is young and inexperienced, but she is also tender of heart and giving of spirit. These qualities will not only honor her Goddess, but will also guide her in her craft."

"Please, Cynara, when we are alone, call me Ava. We have far too much history together to be formal. So, have you a plan for how this can all be mended and how we might restore some peace to the House? Also, I know Brenna and Caolyn are friends, but I fear Brenna is far too used to having her own way. It will not be beneficial to have her anger affect the Chieftain. Should that happen, I will have to deal with him and that, is never an easy task."

"Ava, I have several ideas regarding the wish gone wrong, but first I have something to tell you. You must hear what we encountered on our way to the House. I fear there are strange things afoot in our midst."

"By the Goddess, tell me Cynara!"

"On our travels from the Great Wood, twice I heard a voice warning me to be '*on guard.*' I did not recognize the voice, but it sounded faintly familiar. The first time it was accompanied by a darkening of the sky and a rising of the wind. The next time, I was attempting to rest in the back of the cart while Caolyn was driving on the road. I was fitful in my sleeping. I thought I was dreaming and cried out during my rest. I frightened Caolyn and told her it was my age and wandering mind. I fear she did not believe me."

Ava looked intently at Cynara while she explained the story. She closed her eyes for a moment and then spoke. "Something is happening that is cause for worry. Have you angered anyone or has there been a recent death that you attended to and perhaps an unrestful spirit about?"

"No, Ava, nothing of the sort. I am wondering if because of the wish gone wrong, the Goddess of Wishes is warning Caolyn of something to come. But why would she speak to me and not Caolyn?" Cynara's face was full of worry as she spoke.

"No, I do not think it is the Goddess of Wishes, but I do think it is a spirit of some sort. Perhaps the spirit feels it easier to work through you. We will all watch for the signs in the next several days. Perhaps we should weave a protection spell around Caolyn, just to be safe. Now what is the discovery you made in the village? I am always happy to be aware of village happenings. "

"Oh, Ava, while traveling through the village an old and unkempt man called my name. I turned and could not recognize him, but he surely knew me. Then he exclaimed. 'It is I Drest!"

"WHAT! DREST! You saw Myra's brother?" Ava jumped to her feet. "But we all thought he had passed to the other world. How can it be!?"

"Yes, I felt the same, Ava. I made Caolyn stop the wagon and I went to him. While I was scolding Drest for his unkempt appearance and yet hugging him as a long-lost friend; he caught sight of Caolyn and called out 'Myra' and collapsed. I bade Caolyn to bring water and begged the Goddess not to lose him now. When he awoke, he saw Caolyn and began calling her Myra again. He exclaimed that he must be in the other world if he was seeing his beloved sister, but Caolyn explained who she was and a broad smile spread across his face."

"This is strange and wonderful news! Where has he been? Why did he not return to us before now? Where is he staying?" Ava asked excitedly.

Cynara explained that he had been staying in his old home that was in great disrepair. She went on to tell that she had given him her symbol to bring to the Chieftain and ask for refuge as an old warrior. "I bade him to clean himself and to nourish his body with good food at the Chieftain's home. I told him we would seek him out and bring him to the House once you granted permission."

Ava sat down and shook her head. "There are many things happening, Cynara. I think there is more than mere circumstance going on. We will have to pray to the Goddess for guidance and be watchful of all that is happening. I will leave it to your wisdom when to bring him here. I will await his coming with great expectation. Perhaps he has an important part in all that is coming to be. What a night this has been. I am weary, dear friend. I feel we both will do well with some rest. I bid you good night."

Cynara stood up to leave but not without taking gifts from her bag. "Here is some lavender and blueberry tea I have brought from my garden. Perhaps your maid servant can prepare it for you. It will help you to rest. Here also are some freshly dried and mashed berries to sweeten your food and mint tea. Good night, Ava. It is good to be home."

"Thank you, dear friend," Ava responded.

XI

After bidding Lady Ava a good night, Cynara made her way to the sleeping chamber. Because of her status as a healer and a wise woman, she was given a chamber to herself. She was glad to have some time to be alone. As she entered the chamber a young maid was waiting and asked if she would need anything. Cynara looked about and saw the hearth was lit and a small pot was steaming on the fire. She was thinking of chamomile and lavender tea for herself. "No child, I am fine. Take your leave and have a restful night." The young maid nodded and smiled as she turned to leave the room.

"Now for my tea," Cynara thought. "It has been a long and strange day. Thank the Goddess that Ava was more than kind and gentle with Caolyn. In the next few days, while Caolyn is working out her time of punishment, I must begin to untangle the wish gone wrong. I also must meet this Ronan fellow. I will need to discover his intentions with regard to courting Caolyn, and then see about a meeting with Ava and Drest. It will be a busy several days." Cynara walked to the hearth, found a wooden cup and, after placing her tea leaves in the cup, poured a good measure of steaming water.

"Now to settle on this fine bed and drink my tea," she sat on the feather bed.

Meanwhile, in the community sleeping chamber, Caolyn had settled in for the night. The House was quiet and peaceful. It felt wonderful after the bumpy road trip and the many events of the day. She was glad that Lady Ava had been generous when meeting out her punishment. She offered a prayer to the Goddess and drifted off to sleep.

The three days Caolyn spent with Nora passed quickly. It was enjoyable to spend time with Brian as well. Caolyn could see that Nora and Brian were smitten with each other. They playfully teased each other back and forth during the day's work. Caolyn took note that Brian was also very considerate of Nora, trying to find ways to assist her whenever possible. He was loath to leave Nora, and she often had to usher him out in order to keep privacy for the women and young maids who came to use the bathing pool.

On the last day of Caolyn's punishment, Nora and she were enjoying their lunch in the garden just outside the Chamber of Waters. "So," Caolyn began, "I shall miss our time together Nora. It has been a great pleasure for me to assist you these three days."

"For me as well, I am so used to having my younger kin about that I am often lonely in this task, but having you hear these past three days has helped me feel a little less lonely. It also makes me smile when Brian finds time to come about and help."

Caolyn looked at Nora, who was smiling from ear to ear. "So, Brian chases away the loneliness, does he?"

"Yes, he does but sometimes he is too much under foot, and I must shoo him away. The work is not hard and I have much free time, unlike my time on the farm. There, I never seemed to have any time to myself and I often begged my Mam for it. Now, there are times I would give anything to hug my little sisters and brothers.

"Would you like for me to ask Lady Ava if you could be spared some time away to visit your family? Caolyn asked.

"Oh, Caolyn! Could you? I would be ever grateful!"

"I could, but first let me see what my Auntie has learned with regards to how we might fix the wish that went wrong. I fear that until it is made right, Lady Ava will be in no hurry to grant me any favors."

"I can wait, Caolyn, just knowing that you might find a way for me to see my kin would be a great favor. I will pray to the Goddess for your success, and I will try to use my gift of fey to see if the future holds a visit home." Nora rushed to hug Caolyn.

The remainder of their last day together passed quickly, and by midday there were no bathers to be helped in the Chamber or bathing pool. The two friends began gathering up the various oils, drying cloths and soaps that had been used that day. Their chores were interrupted by a shout of, "Hello, my Ladies!" They turned to see Brian entering the Chamber.

"Well Master Brian, have you come to help us finish cleaning or have you come for sweet talk with Nora?" Caolyn teased. She looked from Nora to Brian and both of them were blushing like the red roses of summer.

"I have come for a bit of both, Caolyn, and I have been asked by your Auntie to come and bid you to go to her chamber in the sleeping quarters. She bid me tell you she has information for you that is most important. Perhaps she has found a love potion for Ronan."

"I see it is now your turn to be the teaser, young sir," Caolyn answered.

"Brian," Nora chimed in, "never mind teasing Caolyn. You have delivered the message; now come. I have some heavy carts full of things to be cleaned and stored away. You can assist me with the task. Come along, please," Nora said biting back a smile.

Brian knew when Nora meant business and when he must attend to the task. He gave a wink to Caolyn and ran toward Nora, "My Lady needs me," he chuckled.

"Nora, am I free to take my leave of you on this our last day together?" Caolyn asked.

Nora nodded her head in response. "Then come, let me give you a sisterly embrace. I have never had a little sister, and I feel in our three days together we have become like sisters. Know that you may seek me out at any time for help and guidance as you learn to follow the rules of the House and the path that has been chosen for you." Caolyn bent over and hugged Nora tightly.

"I wish you well in fixing your bad wish, Caolyn. I, too, feel as if I now have an elder sister, someone to help me along the way. It is good to know you are in the House."

"Nora, come on, I have little time to help you," Brian began. "If I am too long away from the stables, one of the ladies or guardians of the House will be soon after me."

XII

The two maidens parted, and as Nora ran to Brian, she could be heard giving him orders. Caolyn smiled to herself as she watched them walk away together. Two waifs trying to find their path in the world. The House would be a good haven for both of them. She turned toward her aunt's chamber. As she walked along, she was hoping that Cynara had found a way to fix the wish. She also smiled remembering what Brian had said about Ronan and a love potion. Perhaps Cynara had met him by now, and perhaps there was a way he could court her. "What will be, will be," she thought.

Reaching Cynara's chamber, Caolyn found the door ajar. She could see the late afternoon sun lighting the inside. Cynara seemed to be humming a familiar tune, but Caolyn could not remember where she had heard it. She shrugged her shoulders, and knocked on Cynara's door, and called, "Auntie, are you there?"

"Come in, come in, Caolyn, I have been waiting for you most of the afternoon. I was hoping you would be here before the evening repast so that I might tell you all that has happened while you were with Nora." Cynara was smiling broadly and greeted Caolyn with a loving hug.

"Auntie, I was hoping that you would have news to share about the mending of the wish gone wrong and perhaps some news about Ronan," Caolyn responded. "I have been kept busy with Nora and have learned much about taking care of the needs of others. She and I have become fast friends in the three days. She has a quick mind and learns things quite easily."

"Yes, yes, my dear. We can discuss the young miss another time. Sit by the hearth; I have much to tell you." Cynara spoke while waving Caolyn to the stool by the hearth. Caolyn sat as she was told and waited for her Auntie to settle in a large oak chair filled with feather-stuffed pillows. The size of the chair seemed to make Cynara look like a small child as she sat in it.

"Now, my dear," Cynara began, "Lady Ava and I discussed much in the past three days. I described our meeting with your long lost Uncle Drest. She was as shocked as I that he was still alive. However, he is not our main concern at this time. It seems that Brenna is still being pursued by more young warriors none of whom she wants, and not by Ronan, who she does want with all her being."

"Auntie, did you get to meet Ronan?"

"Yes, dear, I will get to that, but first, hear me out," Cynara continued. "In all our discussion, Ava remembered that there is a wishing stone a day's ride from the House. The stone is said to be more powerful than using a well for casting a wishing spell. The place is called Iar Connacht. It is bound by the sea on one side, and there are many lakes about it. It is on this land that, in days past, a giant tried to take over the villages nearby. He was fierce and destroyed all and any in his way. Arawen, one of the gods of war and revenge, was so angered by the giant's behavior that he caused a great shaking of the earth. In response, the giant grabbed a huge pointed rock and slammed it into the earth. Legend says that Arawen caused the earth to swallow the giant, and to this day, the giant's hand that was turned to stone still remains visible above the earth. Over time, those who went to see the site of the giant's hand also saw the large, pointed stone now forever standing as tall as the giant. Legend has been passed come down saying the stone has the power to grant wishes. It is said, if one can stand with their back to the stone and toss a pebble smoothed by the sea over the peak, their wish will be granted. The people of Iar Connacht believed that this was Arawen's gift to them for having suffered under the giant's rule. Perhaps invoking Caolinn, the Goddess of Wishes and using the stone will give your wish the power to be made right. We can plan a trip to the stone while the summer season is still with us and with the Goddess' help make this right, Caolyn."

"But, Auntie, is there any way that we can make it right and not have Ronan's feelings turned to Brenna?"

"Caolyn, first let us fix the wish and stop the constant flow of young warriors at the Chieftain's house. This is not the time to worry about Sir Ronan. We must put our efforts in to mending this wish gone wrong. Cynara could see by Caolyn's expression that this was not what she wanted to hear, but it was the right decision.

"I trust your wisdom, Auntie. You are right. This must be fixed! I do have a request though. If this place is near Nora's home, can she accompany us? I promised I would try to find a way to have her visit her family. She does not let it show, but she misses them so."

"I will seek Lady Ava's permission for this. I see no

reason why she could not go with us if we are traveling near her home. Perhaps her family would give us shelter for one night during the trip. Her gift of fey may also be beneficial to us. They say the land out that way is one of magic and spiritual power. We shall see. Come, walk with me to the evening meal, so we can continue our talk."

Caolyn stood up to assist Cynara from her chair. The two started toward the door just as the bells for the evening meal chimed. Caolyn's hopes were high that the wish could be corrected and that she and Ronan could find their way to each other.

XIII

When the evening ritual was over, Caolyn started toward the community sleeping chamber. Her mind was crowded with so many thoughts. She feared she would not get much sleep that night. When worked with Nora, she had kept busy and her body needed rest at the end of the day so thoughts were easily pushed aside for sleep. This was not so this night, and she knew she would be restless.

While walking through the long passage way to her bed, she passed the door to the younger maidens' sleeping chamber. "Perhaps Nora is about," she thought. She stepped inside and smiled at the youngest of the maidens who were already fast asleep. She thought about how at peace they looked and wished she could have a younger, freer mind again. As her eyes adjusted to the darkness, she saw Nora chatting softly with several maidens of about her age. Just then Nora turned and ran to her. Whispering, Nora began, "Caolyn, I knew I would see you this night. I was wondering when you would come." Caolyn and Nora embraced.

"Did you see my coming?"

"Yes, and I also saw us on the road to my kin's farm. When do we leave?" Nora could hardly contain her excitement.

Caolyn took Nora's hand and led her to the door of the chamber so they could speak without other ears to listen. "Nora, how can that be? Auntie was only going to speak to Lady Ava after prayers. There cannot be a decision made yet!"

"But, Caolyn, I saw us this afternoon. I was watching the sun sink into the ground and there in the distance I saw Cynara, you, myself, Brian, and a guardian warrior I do not know on the road. What I do not understand is why so many of us will be traveling. The way to my kinfolks' farm is not a dangerous path. Why are we not traveling, just the three of us?"

"Cynara was to ask if you could accompany us on a journey to the place called Iar Connacht. It is said that there is a powerful wishing stone there where wishes have a better chance of coming true. She was to ask Lady Ava, if it were near your home, that you be allowed to accompany us on the journey. You are amazing my little 'sister!' Do you know of this place?"

"I have heard Iar Connacht a land of great beauty and magic. I have also heard the lakes of the region have water spirits and hags, but I have not heard of the wishing stone. Perhaps this is why we need a warrior with us, but for what reason must Brian attend?" Nora asked.

"I do not know Lady Ava's reasoning, but tomorrow when I hear all the details, perhaps I will understand. As for now, the hour grows late and you must be about your morning chores early, so off to bed with you." Caolyn hugged Nora and returned to the passageway with another thought added to the many that weighed on her mind.

"Caolyn," Nora softly called. "I'm going to see my kin, thank you."

"Do not give your thanks too early, sweet Nora. There is much about this trip that is unknown. With Cynara's wisdom, your growing gift of fey, and a warrior to travel with us, I hope all will be made right. I fear that this misguided wish has caused so many disruptions for everyone. Good night." Caolyn waved as she turned and walked away.

Nora did not tell Caolyn that she had a bit of an uneasy feeling come over her when she mentioned lar Connacht. She did not know the place, but she had heard stories and not all of them were good. "Please, Goddess, I ask that my gift may be helpful to my friends and those that we meet when we travel. I thank you for the blessing of a journey home, Nora whispered as she climbed into her bed.

In her bed, Caolyn quietly waited for sleep. Her mind was even more troubled. The one bright spot was that perhaps Ronan might be the warrior that accompanied them. In spite of all that was on her mind, she invoked the Goddess' protection for what was ahead and soon fell asleep.

XIV

The morning sun entered the sleeping chamber windows and soon there was much activity about the space. Caolyn yawned and stretched out on her bed. She was surprised that she had slept so well. Before rising she turned toward the sun, bowed her head to her chest and thanked the Goddess for her restful sleep and for the beautiful sunrise. She then turned, got up, straightened out her sleeping space, and went off to prepare for the day and to break fast. She knew this day held many decisions for Lady Ava. Would she allow Nora to travel with them? Who would be the warrior chosen as their guardian on the trip? What plans would have to be made for the trip? What would they take to ease their journey? Her head was spinning as she strode outside to the courtyard and went to the kitchen for something to eat.

On her way to the kitchen, she saw Brian waving and coming toward her. "Mistress Caolyn," he called. "Have you a moment?"

"For you, Master Brian? Always! What are you up to on this glorious morn?"

"Have you heard? I am to accompany you and your auntie on a journey." Brian was smiling from ear to ear as he spoke.

"Are you sure, Brian? I thought we were to have a warrior accompany us on this journey? I am somewhat confused."

"You are to have me and a warrior to act as guardian. I am to accompany you because I might be needed as a lookout during the journey. I heard your auntie and Lady Ava speaking about the trip as they broke fast."

"Brian, how many times must I warn you not to listen to conversations, especially the Lady's. You will run out of luck one day, my lad of the big ears." Caolyn scolded and teased.

"Aw, Caolyn, I hide well, and besides, how can I learn anything if I don't eavesdrop?"

"Well, I hope that you are well hidden, but nonetheless, it is wrong. You did not happen to hear which warrior might be our protector on this journey, did you?"

"No but are you hoping it is Ronan?" Brian teased.

"No, what will be will be, but I wouldn't mind if he accompanied us," Caolyn responded blushing like a red rose. "Be off with you now. I am hoping to hear from my Auntie this morn about the journey. I will seek you out when I know more. How will I ever survive a journey with you underfoot!" Caolyn laughed as she gently shooed Brian on his way.

Caolyn continued to the kitchen. She did not mention the possibility of Nora also going on the journey. "Auntie and I will have our hands full with those two if Nora is allowed to come," she thought. "May the Goddess give us patience, safety and counsel on this journey."

Caolyn went about getting her morning meal. She

sat with several other young maidens to eat. She had not had much conversation with her sisters in the house since before all the wishing problems began.

"Caolyn, how good to see you," said Moraid. "We have all missed you at the gatherings where our studies are conducted."

"We have heard many rumors about you Caolyn," said Hannah, one of the other maidens.

"Indeed," Caolyn began. "I am sure there are many rumors about, and for sure there is truth within some of them. I am asking all of you to be kind with regard to my reputation. I have been disciplined by Lady Ava for my wrong doings, and with the help of my auntie, I hope to fix any wrong doings."

"So, is it true that you tried to make a wishing spell and that it went terribly wrong?" Moraid asked.

"Yes, I am afraid I have turned many things upside down for many people. I thought I was only helping a friend, but my inexperience proved costly."

All of the girls were listening intently hoping to hear more information about the rumors of the Chieftain's daughter Brenna being the main object of the misguided wish. Caolyn did not want to discuss any of the details of the wish, nor any of the things that had happened as a result.

"Please forgive me, my friends," Caolyn went on. "I fear speaking of this will only cause more confusion and I do not want anything else to go wrong. Once all this is behind me, I promise I will tell all of you everything. Perhaps my mistake can be a learning tool for all of us. One thing is sure, do not be too quick to think we have learned enough about our craft to function alone. I know now I should have sought guidance from one of our teachers or even my auntie." Caolyn rose to her feet to leave.

"We will pray to the Goddess for your success," Moraid called to Caolyn.

"Thank you my sisters. Pray also that I will have the courage to get this right."

XV

Caolyn was off to find Cynara and see if any details of the journey had been decided. The sooner they could start, the sooner it would be done. She walked out of the kitchens to the courtyard. The sun was shining brightly, and birds were singing their summer songs. She could not help but smile at the brightness of the day. She thought how lovely it would be to go to the stables and have Brian get a horse ready for her so she could ride out into the countryside, but there was much to be done.

As she started toward the door to the House, she could see Cynara in the herb garden that was just beyond the courtyard. "She must be gathering supplies for the journey," she thought. Cynara turned, saw her and waved for her to come forward.

"Caolyn, I was gathering several herbs to take with us on our journey. Come, I have much to tell you and you can help with the gathering. You will be pleased to know, Lady Ava has consented to allow Nora to travel with us."

"I know, Auntie, Nora told me last evening when I saw her in the sleeping chambers."

Cynara laughed and shook her head, "The young maid saw the journey, did she not? I also advised Ava that Nora's gift would be helpful to us. She will be a good guide as well as she is from that part of the land."

"She did see us Auntie and she saw Brian and an unknown warrior as well. Are you aware that we will be such a large group?"

"Yes, my dear, Brian can manage the cart and heavy things we will need, and the warrior will need his help with the horse and mule. Now, before you ask, Ronan is the warrior that will be with us. I have an uneasy feeling about his presence, but Lady Ava assures me he is trustworthy and of the highest character. I must have your sincere promise that courting will be at the bottom of the list until the wish is made right. Do you give your word?"

Caolyn was very excited that Ronan would be coming, but she did not let her feelings show. This was an important journey. Nora had spoken of stories from Lar Connaught that were troubling, and she knew she must have her wits about her when fixing the wish. "I promise, Auntie. I will be attentive to the purpose of our journey."

"Good, we leave at tomorrow's first light. Today will be a day of preparation. Go and find Miss Nora and Master Brian. I have been assured by Lady Ava and the Master of the Stables that they will be given time to help us prepare for the journey. As for Ronan, a messenger has been sent to the Chieftain's abode to gain permission for his presence. I want to have most everything ready by his arrival so that time can be spent making him aware of his duties. Now go along and bring the two young souls to me so we can prepare."

"I am off, Auntie. Where shall we meet for the preparations?"

"Meet me by the door to the place where supplies for the House are accepted. There will be much we can accomplish in that area. Tell Brian and Nora to bring what they will need on the journey. I must inspect everything. Also, tell Brian to bring one of the large sturdy wagons and make sure he knows which mule will be best suited for the work." Cynara turned and went back to gathering the plants she would need.

"Yes, Auntie, I will do those things and meet you soon," Caolyn smiled as she went off to the bathing chamber to fetch Nora. "Auntie has a bit of a warrior in her spirit," Caolyn thought. "She is good at giving commands." Caolyn hurried on her way.

Shortly after Caolyn left, a young lass from the House came out to Cynara. "Mistress, I have been sent by the guard at the gate to bid you come. You have a visitor."

"I have a visitor, little one? Would they be a mistress or a man?"

"He is a very old man, a grandfather to be sure, Lady," the young lass responded. "He surely has many years like you."

Cynara chuckled, "Ah yes, I do have many years little one. Be off, go and tell the guard I will soon come."

As the young lass curtsied and ran off, Cynara thought the visitor must be Drest come back for a visit. She had nearly forgotten about meeting him on the day they arrived in the village. So much had happened since that day. "If he is here, he must be feeling well," she thought. "I hope he will understand that I cannot give him much time today."

Cynara wrapped the herbs she had been gathering in a sack cloth and placed them on a table in the sun to dry. She then went toward the gate to see Drest.

Drest saw her approaching. He walked toward her waving and smiling. Cynara thought how much better he looked. He was clean, his hair and beard neatly combed and groomed. He even looked as if he might have had a few good meals.

"Cynara," Drest called. "I took your advice and have spent time with the Chieftain. He was more than welcoming. He said I must be one of the oldest warriors in the village and surrounding countryside."

"Drest, my dear old friend, it is good to see you well and steady on your feet once again. Come, we will go into the kitchen and have the cook make us something. It is past my midday repast and I could use some tea."

As the two were walking to the kitchen, the same lass who had given Cynara the message of Drest's arrival came toward them. She curtsied and said, "The Lady Ava has heard of the old warrior's arrival and she sent me to bid you go to her chamber for a small repast."

"Who are you calling an 'old warrior'?" Drest teased the little one.

"I am sorry, sir," the lass began. "Lady Ava said that you were a warrior once, but to me you look like a grandfather. I meant no disrespect."

"Surely, it would be a joy to be a grandfather," Drest replied. "And never be afraid to speak the truth. I am well on in years. Tell Lady Ava I accept her invitation and am honored."

The little lass turned to run off to Lady Ava's chamber, but then, she stopped suddenly and turned. "Will you be long, Grandfather, because you walk slowly?" she asked.

Drest and Cynara both laughed. "What is your name, little one?" Drest asked.

"'T'is Annie," she responded.

"Annie, a fine name," Drest replied. "Tell the Lady I will be quick. I am old but I can still walk at a good pace."

"I will, Grandfather," Annie curtsied.

"That little one has a cheerful character, does she not, Cynara? It is good to have little ones about. It makes me long for days gone past."

"She is cheerful and has a sweet countenance," Cynara responded. "One of the things I have enjoyed most about the House is the company of those who are young and full of energy. Of course, there are times when the energy exceeds my strength. Then I am grateful that I have a private chamber to retreat to."

The two old friends continued to chat as they walked toward their meeting with Lady Ava.

"Come in, Come in!" Lady Ava called as she saw her friends approaching. She walked towards them smiling. "Drest, you have returned to us! We all feared you long gone and on to the land of the gods."

"Ava, so good to see you. The gods do not want my old bones quite yet, I must say, though, it is not for lack of my trying to leave this world. There have been days that I would have thrown myself over the ledges, but something always held me back."

"Perhaps your wisdom is still needed at this time. We are glad you have found your way to us. Come sit and we will talk and enjoy a small meal together," Ava said moving toward the garden and a lovely area to sit and be warmed by the golden sunlight.

Once the small group was seated, the conversation focused on Drest and what had happened to him once he had left the village after the death of Myra, his sister and Caolyn's mother. "I was a lost and broken man for so long," Drest began. "I should have stayed and been a presence in Caolyn's life, but I knew she was where Myra would have wanted her, here in the House that she so loved. I had plans to go again and find the man that sired Caolyn to make him aware he had a child, but each time I would start to go, I was overcome with sadness. I also had large a wound on my back and my sword arm had lost its strength. I was broken inside and out, a warrior no more. What good could I be to anyone if I was not good for myself." Drest's old eyes were misted over with memories.

"But now you are back with us, and you can share memories of Myra with Caolyn. Memories no one has of her but you." Cynara gently squeezed the arm of her friend.

"Drest," Lady Ava began. "We are glad you are with us again, and we will find a way to make you feel useful and valued. You did well in the battle to save the House and many lives the night of the attack of the northern tribes. Make peace with it. As for now, we have much to tell you about a journey about to take place."

Cynara quickly cut in on the conversation. "Drest, on the day we saw you in the village, Caolyn had been to my home in the west woods. She was distraught. She had made a wish for her friend, Brenna, daughter of the Chieftain, but the wish had gone wrong, and she wants to make the wish right. She attempted to have the favors of a young warrior be bestowed on Brenna, but the young warrior has found favor with Caolyn and many unwanted warriors have been seeking Brenna."

A big grin spread across Drest's face. "Indeed, I have seen the results of the wish. I must confess I did not know the reason for all of the would-be suitors at the Chieftain's home, but it has greatly upset the daughter, and many of the young lads are walking about like moonstruck fools. The Chieftain's Captain of the Guard is having a most difficult task keeping the lads in line with the discipline needed for training as warriors."

"The Chieftain has informed me of all the problems at his camp," Lady Ava said. "I have assured him that we are about the work of making this right. This is part of the reason for the journey I am about to explain. Cynara, Caolyn, as well as Nora and Brian, two of our young charges, will accompany each other on the journey. Ronan, a most trusted warrior, I have been told, will also travel with them for protection. They are to travel to the western lakes and sea, the area known as lar Connaught, with its' large wishing stone said to have great power. It is there we hope to correct the wish gone wrong."

"Lar Connaught, that is an area of great beauty and at times great danger," Drest commented. "Often, men wandered too far from the lines of their fellow warriors would not return. It is said that the Sirens of the sea tricked them to a watery grave. I know of the stone from fireside stories, but I have never seen it. Would you need me to go as well?"

"No," Cynara began, "our group is large enough. We want to be on our way back to the House in three days. Young Nora has the gift of fey which will be helpful and her kin folk live that way. She has not seen them for a long time. She will help us and visit them, though this is not a trip for pleasantries. It is to be one of accomplishment."

The conversation was interrupted by the young maid Annie who entered the garden. "Lady, I was asked to tell you a young warrior is here to be told of the task he is to do for you." Annie looked toward the group and could not help herself when she saw Drest. She started toward him and stopped.

"Come along, Little One, "Drest beckoned.

Annie took a step, but stopped and turned her face toward Lady Ava. "Good lass, Ava began. "Now what must you do?"

"I must wait for your response Lady and I can go only with your permission," Annie responded.

"You are learning well. Go bid hello to Drest and then return to the warrior and bid him come to us," Ava smiled.

Annie ran to Drest and threw her arms around his neck. "Did you enjoy your food, Grandfather? I helped in the kitchen."

Drest's face broke into the warmest of smiles as he greeted the little lass. "Yes, I did but not as much as I am enjoying seeing you again. Now hurry along you have a message to deliver. I will see you before I depart." Annie smiled, curtsied to Lady Ava and ran off.

"That one is a charmer already," Ava chuckled. "She will do well finding her way in the world."

XVI

While the group waited for Ronan's arrival they finished their midday meal. Ronan entered the garden and bent his head toward the Lady out of respect for her. He looked toward Drest and Cynara, thinking "If these elders are going to be on the trip, it will be made at a slow pace."

"Come, Ronan, take your rest here in the garden while I explain the task you are about to do and the need for your assistance," Lady Ava gestured toward a seat for the young warrior. "Do you know Cynara, Caolyn's "auntie" and Drest, one of our eldest warriors; he is also Caolyn's blood uncle. He has been the guest of the Chieftain recently."

Ronan moved toward the bench offered to him while responding to Lady Ava's question. "I have heard of the wise woman, Cynara, and know of her kinship to Caolyn. As for Sir Drest, I have met him and enjoyed time with him at the Chieftain's table." Ronan nodded toward both elders.

"Be seated, young lad," Drest began. "I have met you and have heard of the great respect that the Chieftain has for you and your abilities, especially the ability as a great swimmer."

"Thank you, Drest. The Chieftain holds you in regards as well. Many of the young warriors have begun to hear of some of your battle excellence and bravery in defending the village and the House in days gone by."

Up to this point, Cynara had merely been taking the whole scene in. She had heard of Ronan's abilities as a warrior and of his excellent character, but there was still something about him that may her hold opinion.

"Cynara, would you like to explain to Ronan what this journey is to be about and why we need his services?" Lady Ava asked.

"It is good to finally meet you and see you in the flesh, Ronan" Cynara began.

"I have been looking forward to meeting you as well, my Lady." Ronan replied with a respectful nod.

"This is to be a very quick journey. We must travel to Iar Connaught to find the powerful wishing stone to make right a wish that has gone wrong. This wish has caused many lives to be turned upside down. Once the wish is changed, we will return to the house. I do not see this trip taking more than three days. There will be no time for any side journeys or any feasting. Do you understand?"

"Yes, Lady," Ronan replied. "May I ask who is to be on the journey?"

"The travelers are to be Caolyn, the stable boy Brian and Nora one of the young maidens in the house, along with me of course. Nora has the gift of fey and her home is on route to Iar Connaught. Her family will provide us shelter for one night. Do you have any thing you would like to know?" Cynara asked.

"I have some concerns. Legend has it that Iar Connaught is a land of great danger. We will have to be on our guard when traveling through that area, and we should spend as little time as possible there. If we had a smaller group, we could make better time," Ronan explained.

"I am aware, young sir, but nonetheless this is the best way to reverse the wish. Surely you are aware that the Chieftain is unhappy with the manner in which this wish has come to pass," Cynara went on. As she looked into Ronan's face she saw a slight smirk. "You find this amusing, Ronan?" Cynara said raising her voice.

"If you will pardon my amusement, dear lady, I was just thinking about some of the young warriors acting as if they had been put under a spell of love. There are days the captains find it difficult to keep order. I do not find the results of the wish amusing," Ronan replied.

"Ronan," Lady Ava interrupted, "be assured that Cynara has many talents that will be of assistance on the journey. Brian was chosen because he does well with the horses and can do many menial tasks that will be of value to the group. Nora's gift will help you to be alerted before danger is too close, and she has earned a trip to see her kin. As for Caolyn, she is responsible for the wish gone wrong, and she must set it right. She is a namesake of Caolainn, Goddess of Wishes, and so must do homage to her by setting the wish right."

"I have offered to come as well," Drest began, "but Cynara assures me that they will be well protected with you as their guardian. You are traveling with two of my most treasured people, please take heed to keep them and all of you protected."

"Lady Ava, Cynara and Drest be assured I will do my best to provide protection and security for all so that we will be safely returned to home. Now, if I may have leave to go, there is much to prepare for the journey. I will be here at the first light, ready to begin." Ronan stood up and bowed in respect to the group.

"Ronan, please wait for me a moment outside the garden gate," Lady Ava rose from her seat.

Turning to Drest and Cynara she said, "You may both take your leave my friends. I am sure there is much to prepare before tomorrow's journey. Drest, do not be a stranger. You are always welcome at the House." Ava gave them both a gentle hug and left to speak to Ronan,

"She is warning him there is to be no attempt at courting on this trip, I hope." Cynara said a bit sharply. "I will not have the time nor the patience to be dealing with matters of the heart. We must be about the business we have set out to do and then return home safely."

"Cynara, Ronan has the recommendation of the Chieftain, what more can you ask?"

"Drest, I cannot explain it, but I have an uneasy feeling about the young man. Perhaps it is just worrying about the outcome of the journey. Once we are back, if he wants to court Caolyn, we can make an arrangement. You must be part of that as you are her only blood relative."

"I will be waiting for your return and then you and I can discuss any courtship of Caolyn and all things that must be considered."

"Good, let us go, for I have much to do. The two left the garden by a different gate so as not to disturb Ronan and Ava.

As they were walking, Drest asked, "Does Ronan remind you of anyone from the past? Do you know his sire or mother?"

"No, Drest, but I am not one to ask. Like you I have been long away from the House and village. There are not many of my former maidens here at the House. Many have been married away or like me sought the quiet of the woods or mountains. And, like Myra, many dwell with the Goddess," Cynara said wistfully.

"It is nothing. I just sense something familiar about him. Perhaps he is kin to a fellow warrior long past," Drest said as he gently took Cynara's arm as they walked.

XVII

In the garden, Ronan stood waiting patiently for the Lady Ava to come. He was mulling over all the things he had just heard about this upcoming journey. His primary thought was, "Why me? Surely a warrior with less experience could have been chosen for this? It seems to be such a small task. Fixing wishes! At least Caolyn will be present on the journey. Perhaps, there will be time to make my intentions known. How much protection and scouting will be required of me?"

While he was lost in his thoughts, Lady Ava had come and her voice shook him back to the present. "Ronan, young sir, I have a few words of instruction for you before you depart."

"Yes, Lady," Ronan responded, bowing his head in respect. "I will heed your instructions."

"Do not think that this is a small task you are undertaking, Ronan. Cynara and I are as close as two kinswomen can be without being blood bound. As for Caolyn, she has grown up in the House without a mother, and she could not be dearer to Cynara and me than our own flesh and blood could be.

"Be assured that your strength and warrior wisdom could be needed at any turn on this journey. Do not take my word, but ask the Chieftain if I am not correct. The area of Iar Connaught is one of mystery and legend. Many stories have come down through the years of dangerous happenings in the area. Let the Chieftain confirm the story of the giant whose hand turned to stone. Have him confirm that all that is left of him is the hand rising from the ground. He angered the God Arawen, a god of war and revenge. Arawen was the patron protector of the people and land in Iar Connaught. The giant caused such pain to the people they begged for Arawen's help. Arawen is said to have given the giant warning, but he paid no heed. One day Arawen struck down the giant, as he started to rise, the ground shook, the sky darkened and a great storm arose. Thunder bolts rained down on the giant. The earth opened and swallowed him whole. Still, the giant tried to rise. He raised his hand to stop the lightning bolts striking from the sky. The ground shook again as it swallowed giant.

Arawen was seen throwing a huge thunder bolt, which struck the giant's hand and turned it to stone. The hand of stone is all that is left of the giant to this day. So be aware, since that time the area around all of Iar Connaught has been one of mystery and superstition. You will need to keep your wits about you, and not let your heart be the leader of your tasks. Your head and thoughts must be on the journey and bringing all of you home again. Understood!?

"Yes, my Lady," Ronan responded. "You can trust that I will have their safety and security as my first responsibility. Thank you for the information regarding the happening with the giant and the God Arawen. To be sure, I will invoke his protection for the group and ask for his guidance in completing the journey."

"Thank you, young sir. It has not gone unnoticed that you have feelings for Caolyn. Again, I remind you, matters of the heart are not to be of concern at this time. This may not be the kind of battle you are used to waging, but be warned it may be no less dangerous. When you return safely, you can be about your courting of Caolyn, but not now."

"As you wish, my Lady, and now I must take my leave. There is much to prepare, and I will need to consult with the Chieftain before I depart on the journey. I will be here shortly before the first light to secure all things before departure. I give you my word that I will do all I can to return them all safely home," Ronan assured Ava as he bowed and took his leave.

"He is of fine and noble character," Ava thought as she turned to go back to the garden. "I just hope the journey will be without peril. Please Goddess, keep them safe and if danger arises, please let Ronan be as strong as necessary and let the talents of the group assist him when possible."

As she walked toward the garden, the sky darkened and suddenly the wind came up. "Be careful," the wind seemed to whisper. Again came the uneasy feeling that something was afoot. Ava rubbed her shoulders as a chill set in and again she whispered, "Please, Goddess protect them."

XVIII

Cynara and Drest walked through the gardens around the House and toward the stables. It was a beautiful afternoon in midsummer. The sun was still high in the sky and the scent of roses, lavender and herbs from the various gardens filled the air.

"Cynara," Drest began. "Once this journey is over and the Gods find you safely back in the House, what is your plan?"

"My plan? I am not much good at planning, Drest. Why do you ask?"

"Well, surely you must be planning to either stay here at the House or return to your own home in the Great Woods. I am just curious," Drest responded with a small smile.

"Well, to be sure, I would like to return home to the woods. I have a life there and I left behind my old mule Dob. Sometimes I worry that he will be gone when I return. What are your concerns and why are you smiling so?"

"Well, if the gods grant your safe return and you decide to go back to your home, would you enjoy some company on the trip. Surely you do not want to go alone?"

Cynara looked at her friend's weathered face and

noted he was still smiling. Why did her heart flutter when she saw his smile? Perhaps it was that he reminded her of Myra. They have the same smile. "Drest, I had thought I would ask Lady Ava to request an escort for, but I would be happy to have you come along, if you are up to the trip."

"I am and I would so enjoy the time with you and, and......" Drest was now blushing as he stammered.

"Drest, you are blushing like a school boy!" As she spoke, she could feel her own face begin to warm.

Drest began to laugh, "Oh, and what about you!"

Suddenly, they were both laughing and smiling at each other. "Cynara," Drest said with more composure. "We are on in years, but after so much loneliness in my life, I would not mind having the comfort of someone in my later years. Please consider that we may think upon a living arrangement at your home or in the village; whatever makes you happy."

"Drest, I will think on this offer. Once the journey to set the wish right is over and we have all safely returned, we will decide together. I cannot think on it now. My mind is full of all that must be done and set right. You speak the truth. Being alone is tolerable when one is young, but being alone as one walks closer to the end of their time is less tolerable. Thank you, Drest, for speaking," Cynara gently touched Drest's face as she spoke.

"Until you all return, I will be praying to the gods to protect all of you and bring you safely home. God speed Cynara. I will be waiting." Drest leaned forward and gently a kissed on Cynara's forehead. "I am off now, and I will try to find out more about Ronan and why we both have uneasy feelings about such a fine, honorable young warrior."

"Yes, do; this is just one more worrisome burden to carry."

As Drest was walking toward his horse in the stable, he remembered the feelings he had had for Cynara back so many years ago. He never spoke because she was hand-fasted to another. When Cynara was widowed, he was off fighting and later, grieving for his sister and lost in his own self-pity. "Perhaps I have been blessed with another chance for happiness. I pray to the God of Protection, Bran the Blessed, to keep them all safe. I could not bear another tragedy."

His thoughts were interrupted by Brian's voice. "Sir Drest, I have readied your horse. Look who has come to bid you safe journey back to the village." Drest looked up and there was Annie holding a small handful of lavender.

"Oh, my little Miss, you have not forgotten me?" Drest asked with a smile.

"No Grandfather, I have brought you some lavender for your bed. It will give you peaceful rest." Annie reached both her arms up and Drest bent down as Annie threw her arms around his neck. "Will you come to see me again, Grandfather?"

"Yes, little one, I will return and next time I will bring you a gift to thank you for your generous one. I will enjoy the peaceful rest, and think of you as I drift off to sleep. I must go now but I will not be long away."

"I will wait for your return. Goodbye Grandfather." Annie hugged him again.

Brian brought the horse to Drest and helped him up. Drest looked down at Brian and spoke. "Keep your wits about you, young Brian. This may not be an easy journey. You must have the eyes of the hawk and the ears of the fox to be watchful and take warning when necessary. Do you understand?"

"Yes, Sir, I mean to prove myself on this journey. I do not want to be tied to the stables for my life. I will help and be of service to all on the journey."

"Good lad, we will all be invoking the gods for your protection," Drest said as his mount trotted toward the village.

XIX

At the House, the travelers spent the remainder of the day readying for the journey. Brian picked out the best and strongest mule to pull the cart with supplies. He needed a strong cart, but it also had to have enough space for the women travelers to ride when tired, and for Cynara to nap if needed. Brian had been given strict orders by both Cynara and the Stable Master to take only those things that were necessary for the trip. They were to travel as light as possible in order to make good time and be swiftly home.

Brian found a sturdy cart with ample room, and he picked out a young mule with strong- looking haunches. Brian went to the mule and rubbed his muzzle gently, "I am taking you Thorn. You are still young enough to have not become too stubborn, If you work hard, I promise I will find a way to get you a sweet treat at the end of the day. Do you understand?" The mule brayed softly and nuzzled Brian's neck. "Good, Thorn, we understand each other."

Brian then began packing several of the supplies that Cynara, Caolyn and Nora had left for him. He was busy with the task when he heard someone approaching. "Ho Brian," Nora called. "Are you nearly packed for the journey? Have you room for a few more supplies from Cynara?"

"Nora, good day. More! I thought we were to pack light?"

"Well, my dear sir, Cynara says we will need these herbs, oils and teas for the journey. 'Tis a small bundle. I am trying not to jump about with happiness. I am going to see my kin, Brian, and they can meet you as well."

"Alas, I have no kinfolk, Nora. My ma died and my da ran off and left me. I have no sisters or brothers. Lucky for me, the Stable Master knew Da and took me in here, to help with the stables. I have no real sense of family; the House and all within the walls are my family"

Nora ran to hug Brian's neck and took him by surprise. "Brian, it is good that all in the House are your family, but I hope that you will think of me as more than a sister." Nora was holding on to Brian tightly as his face turned a bright crimson.

"So, you two young folk, is the warmth of the summer blossoming love between you as she bursts open the summer flowers?" Caolyn's voice rang out teasingly, breaking the moment between the two young, love-struck people. "You best not be wasting precious time preparing for tomorrow's journey. Be mindful, Auntie will soon be about to check that all preparations are finished before she retires for the night."

Brian and Nora jumped apart, but when they realized it was Caolyn, they both laughed. But Nora soon became serious and pretended to scold Brian. "I told, Brian, did I not, that we had no time for playful games. We must be swift in our work."

Brian rolled his eyes and teased back. "Oh, and who was the one to come and bother me during my tasks? I was doing just fine until you made me stop and find more room for your travel basket, my bossy lady!"

"Enough!" Caolyn spoke, trying to sound older and wiser than the pair. "Cynara has sent me to see that we are indeed all packed and ready to leave at first light. I am to report back before evening prayers. So, are all preparations complete? "

"Yes, Caolyn," Brian began. "The cart is packed; the mule has been fed and bedded for the night. I have packed away all the things that Mistress Cynara has sent to me. The Stable Master has chosen a horse for you to ride. Nora and I will take turns driving the wagon, and Sir Ronan will have his own steed. I believe we are ready."

"Good. Then, Nora, bid good night to Brian as we must be off to evening prayers,"

Caolyn could see by Nora's face she wanted to stay with Brian, but that was not to be on this night. "Come along, Nora, you will be with Brian for three days and you should be well rested for the journey. We want your kin to see that the House and Lady Ava have been good to you. Cynara will also expect that you have taken care to be rested enough to use your gift if the time deems it necessary."

"I am coming, Caolyn," Nora responded as she ran to Brian for a last embrace. "Sleep well, Brian. I will see you at first light."

"As you wish, Lady Nora," Brian chuckled and made a deep bow.

Caolyn watched and thought how lucky they were to find each other so young. "And, as for me, will I find someone who will return my feelings? May it be Ronan, but I fear not. Brenna wants Ronan. The wish was made for her to have her warrior and that warrior is Ronan. I will have to trust the Goddess. All will be done as she sees fit," Cynara mumbled to herself.

Nora ran to her and grabbed her arm. "Come my sister, smile, we are to have a journey!"

"Good eve," both maidens said as they waved to Brian and walked off to evening prayers.

XX

Once the evening prayers and ritual were over, the circle of elder women and maidens, dispersed to their final evening duties and to prepare for the night's rest. When Cynara neared the door to the sleeping chamber, she found Lady Ava and Cynara waiting for her.

"My Lady," Caolyn said bowing respectfully.

"Caolyn," began Lady Ava. "I want you and Cynara to hear my final words before you leave for this journey. It is my hope and wish that this will go smoothly. Cynara has assured me that she has been instructing you on the importance of casting the wishing spell with the utmost of care. This must be made right, Caolyn!"

"Some have thought this mistake to be one of silliness and reason to make fun and games. I assure you it is not. Look beyond the surface. First, you have caused distress to your friend Brenna. The fact that she is the Chieftain's daughter makes it all the worse. Also, having young warriors all acting like love struck fools is neither in the village nor the House's best interest. What if we come under attack and the warriors cannot protect us because of the lack of attention to their duties? This is more serious than silly mooning about! Do you understand?"

Caolyn was struck by the tone of Lady Ava's voice. Never had she spoken to her in such a stern manner. She eyed Cynara eye and could tell that she was also in no mood for gaiety.

"I am aware, my Lady," Cynara said in her most humble voice. "Auntie has spent much time with me since our arrival at the House. I have been made to see where I erred in the performance of the spell. I have been working hard on my strength to stay committed to the task of getting the spell right. I have learned from my namesake, the Goddess Caolainn's lesson. She advises us to pay heed to what we desire and wish for because, once the wish is granted, it might never be undone."

"Good, my child," Ava responded. "I know that your heart was in the right place, but also remember here at the house we pledge to *First Do No Harm.* It is our code. It is of great importance in what we do, how we conduct our lives and how we gain the respect of those we serve. I have the greatest of affection for you, Caolyn, but I must hold you to the same standard as the others. Do you understand?"

"Yes, Lady, I will make this right. I trust in Cynara's wisdom to help me and I have given the task the importance it deserves. I am sorry to have caused such turmoil."

Cynara stepped forward as Lady Ava motioned them both to her. Cynara brought out a white candle that had been lit at the prayer ceremony and placed it on the ground between Caolyn and her. The two women held hands and Lady Ava placed her hands over their heads. "Bow your heads, my cherished ones, and receive the Goddess' protection."

"Goddess of fire, earth, wind and sea
Protect these travelers as they seek to be,
On a journey to make wrong right
Traveling far, keep them in your sight
Let no harm on them or friend fall
Let them return to the House and thee
As I circle round you three
So mote it be"

Ava respectfully circled the women three times continuing to chant the prayer, and then from the pouch on her waist, she removed dried sage, holly leaves and dandelion root and sprinkled it over the flame on the candle. "Please, Goddess," she thought, "may the protection of these powerful plants that you have blessed us with bring my friends and their companions safely back to the House." In addition, her thoughts went to Myra. She bowed her head for a moment and in her heart and thoughts pleaded; "Myra, if you are with the Goddess, please as a mother of this child that you left here with us, please protect her and our friends. In all that is holy, I plead for their safe return."

The candle burned out slowly, and the women gathered up their things, embracing each other and offering words of courage and hope to each other. Quietly, they left for their sleeping chambers with thoughts of what might or might not lie ahead.

XXI

The day for the journey had arrived. The sun's rays were barely breaking when Caolyn rose and hurried to the well for water to wash. She splashed her face and took a long drink. "Now back to get my travel clothes and cape and my leather pouch with wishing herbs. It is best to keep them close to my person on the trip," she thought. "We would not fare well if they were lost."

Back in the sleeping chamber, she quickly dressed and placed the leather pouch around her neck and under her garments. She gathered her travel cloak and her Athame. "I am not sure that I will need this ritual knife on the journey. After hearing all the talk of Iar Connaught and it being a dangerous land, it may be useful to take along," she thought. "The more tools we have the better," she said aloud as she went off to the stables.

When Caolyn arrived, everyone had gathered to do the last preparations. She noticed another warrior, but she was unable to tell who he was and thought, "I hope we are not adding to the travelers."

"Come, Caolyn, we are nearly ready. We will break fast on the road," Cynara called. As she spoke, the unknown warrior turned and smiled at Caolyn. It was Aedan, Ronan's trusted friend.

"Good morn, Caolyn," Aedan began. "I kept company with Ronan to the House and thought it would be good to see you all off. I wish you safe journey."

"Good morn to you as well, Aedan," Caolyn said, walking to the wagon and placing her small bundle inside. "It is kind of you to see us off."

"It is my pleasure. I have brought you some yarrow and mistletoe for courage and protection. I trust you will need both for the journey. You also have Ronan here to protect all of you. As you well know, he is one of our most courageous warriors."

Before Caolyn could answer, Cynara stamped her foot. "Enough! This is not a journey for pleasure! Come, let us be off. Caolyn get to your horse! Nora, Brian, up on the cart and Sir Ronan lead us forward!"

"Thank you, Aedan," Caolyn said running to the horse. Aedan followed and helped her up. Caolyn could see that Aedan wanted to say more, but Cynara was standing in the cart with hands on her hips and a look that could turn a man to stone. Aedan bowed his head, backed away and climbed on his horse.

Cynara sat down and Ronan gave the command to move forward. "Ho, Aedan, we shall see you in three days," Ronan waved to his friend and they were off.

Aedan, stayed watching them go. His thoughts were of Caolyn and how he would like to make his feelings known. He knew he could not as long as Ronan had feelings for her. Ronan was like a brother to him and he could never betray that friendship. "Keep them safe Bran the Blessed," he prayed. "I could not bear to lose either of them. It will be a long three days."

XXII

The day was filled with positive omens, sunshine, beautiful blue sky with only wisps of small clouds scattered about. Brian and Nora happily chatted in the driver's seat of the cart. Cynara, in the back of the cart busied herself reorganizing the various things that had been packed for the journey. On her horse, Caolyn trotted along beside the cart. Ronan rode at the lead.

Caolyn was lost in her thoughts. She was puzzled by what Aedan had said before they departed. "Why, with Ronan there to protect them, would he feel the need to make her a gift of yarrow and mistletoe? Perhaps, he was just being kind, and it made for a good excuse to accompany Ronan on his ride to meet us." She had other thoughts as well, mindful of the fact that this journey could be fraught with danger as well as the completion of a necessary task. She was brought back to the moment by Cynara's voice calling out to her.

"Caolyn, Caolyn! Do you have your wits about you? You seem to be somewhere in the clouds, though there is nary a cloud above us."

"No, Auntie, I am here. I am just thinking about what may or may not lie ahead of us. I am also glad for the blessing of this beautiful day. I guess I am a bit distracted."

"I trust it is not because of yet another young warrior for you to think on," Cynara remarked. "You must stay alert, all of us must, we know not what lies ahead. I hope the remainder of this day will be like the start, and we will arrive at Nora's home in time for the evening meal."

Nora interrupted, having heard the conversation, to say "Mistress Cynara, I see nothing fearful in our path at this time. The journey to my home is usually one of easy going. If the weather stays pleasant, we should, as you have said, be there in time to sup."

"Goddess be praised," Cynara answered. "I will take comfort in knowing you have seen the way clear for us."

Turning to Caolyn, Cynara spoke. "Go up to Ronan at the lead. Tell him we are at his call for when to rest the horses and take our own repast for the midday meal. I trust that he would have broken fast at the Chieftain's dwelling or in the village."

"I will ask him Auntie," Caolyn said as she was thinking that, in all the hurry to be started, she had not had anything to eat since the night before. As she trotted toward the lead, she searched her bag saddled to the horse and found an apple. "After I speak to Ronan, I will allow myself a treat," she thought.

"Ho, Ronan, I have words for you from Cynara."

"Caolyn, I have been waiting to see how much time would pass before I received my travel orders from our 'Captain'." Ronan teased, with a broad grin on his handsome face.

"Ronan, please be patient with Auntie. She has much worry on her mind and it is I that have caused her concerns. She means well and wants this wishing mess to be over and done. I cannot blame her for that. She is asking where we might stop for midday sustenance and how long before we stop?"

"I thought we might stop at the small village known as Caherlistrane. We will be able to rest the horses and have a bit to eat. I spoke with Nora and from there, it is not far to her kin's farm. We should arrive well before the sun is half way to its setting. Please ask Mistress Cynara and see if that meets her favor."

"I am sure she will be fine with your choice, Ronan. I could use a stop because I did not take time to break fast before we left. I will advise Auntie and, if there is any change, I will let you know."

"Caolyn, please, a minute? Would you enjoy spending time riding with me to the village? This may be the most pleasant part of the journey, surely the least dangerous. I would enjoy your company."

"I shall be back, Ronan. I would enjoy the company as well." Caolyn turned back to the wagon, which was moving more slowly than she had realized. Approaching the wagon, she saw Nora raise her finger to her lips and gesture toward the back of the wagon where Cynara was sound asleep. "Good," she thought. "Auntie needs her rest and she may as well take it now. Who knows what the morrow may bring." She pulled her apple out of her pocket and rode back to Ronan.

Ronan was smiling as Caolyn's horse came up alongside of his horse. "We are blessed by the gods to have this day to travel," he said.

"Yes, we are indeed. I hope that the gods and goddess continue to smile on us during this journey."

"Caolyn," began Ronan. "Do you have more knowledge than I with regards to the plans for the outcome of this journey? I am not suggesting that I am not needed, but it seems to me that using a warrior to provide protection to go to a wishing stone and set a wish again, well…."

"Ronan, I may not know much more than you do, but we have been advised by Nora, who is from that way, of the dangers near Iar Connaught. It is said to be a land of mystery and old curses. There are stories of people going near lough Corrib and never returning. I have been told that the wishing stone and the giant's hand that was turned to stone by the God Arawen is the most dangerous place in the entire area. Are you sorry to have been given this task?"

"I am not sorry in the way you would think, Caolyn. I am happy to spend the time with you, though we have not been given official permission to court. I am honoring the commands I have been given. I just feel my talents lie more in the use of my swimming strength and ability to spy on enemies that may come to us by water," Ronan explained.

"Perhaps your swimming talents may be needed near lough Corrib. I have heard from those who have passed by it that it is a large and beautiful lough. In any case, I too am grateful for the chance to know you better."

"We will enjoy our time today and see what the remainder of the journey has in store," Ronan finished.

The little group continued on to Caherlistrane as the sun was reaching its high point in the sky.

XXIII

Back in the village, the same beautiful weather was in place. Drest awoke with plans to accomplish several things. As he stretched out on his cot, his mind was busy mulling over all that had happened in the last two days. He found himself smiling at the thought that Cynara seemed pleased at the possibility of the two of them traveling back to her home in the Great Wood, and perhaps spending their days together. "What a blessing for our advanced age," he thought. "Loneliness is never easy, but it is even more difficult as our days on this ground become less."

Drest left off the pleasant thoughts of Cynara. He knew that he was going to take his leave of the village for a few days. He was planning to travel to the place where Ronan had been a lad and search for any signs of a village or kin to Ronan. Perhaps then, he could learn more about the young warrior. He could not understand why he seemed at times so familiar. "I have seen my share of places and villagers from far and wide," he thought. "Perhaps it is no more than a feeling. I shall break fast and advise the Chieftain that I will take my leave towards the east and see what I can learn." Drest stiffly rose his weary bones up from his sleeping pallet and went out to freshen himself at the well in the village.

Walking toward the well which was half way between the Chieftain's quarters and the warriors' sleeping huts, Drest noticed a young warrior coming in through the west gate.

"Ho, Sir Drest, how are you this fine morn." It was Aedan back from seeing the travelers off.

"I am well, young sir. Aedan, is it? Does my old mind serve me well?

"You are as sharp as a new blade, sir!" Aedan teased.

"Surely you did not have duty at this hour, or are you returning from night watch?" Drest inquired.

"No, my night duty is yet a bit away. I was returning from the House of Maidens. I went with Ronan to see the small group off. Ronan is like a brother to me and I did not mind the task."

"Ah, so they are off and got an early start, good, good." Drest said nodding his head in approval. "I will be praying to the gods for their safety and quick return. It is not a long journey, but has the makings of one of concern because of the land near Iar Connaught."

"Well, if it is any comfort, they have the best warrior in the village as their guide and protector. I would trust Ronan with my life. He has feelings for Caolyn and that will make him all the more alert and protective of them."

"Yes, that is a good thing. About Ronan, do you know how he came to be here in this village? He has no kin here, and I do not believe he was ever captured in a raid as a child."

"No, Sir, Ronan has spoken of being fostered out as a child. I believe his father is still alive, but he speaks little of him. There is some bad blood between them and he does not make his feelings known. He lost his mother at a young age. That is all I know."

"Hmm, a similar story to Caolyn's. Her mother left this earth on her naming day, so she never knew her. Strange how the gods find ways to have us find our way to those who have similar fates. Well, I have taken too much of your time. I must break fast, go to the Chieftain, and advise him I will be gone from the village for a few days myself. Thank you, Aedan, for explaining Ronan's story. May the gods take care of you today," Drest finished as he drew water from the well.

"Have a pleasant day and trip, Sir Drest."

Drest made haste as he readied for the day and had a humble meal of bread and mead. He was then off to seek the Chieftain. On his way to the residence, he noticed a few of the young men still love struck from the wish. They were milling about hoping to see a glimpse of Brenna. He smirked, thinking that none of these poor souls would have a chance with the Chieftain or Brenna In the short time he had been back in the village, he had learned that, if the Chieftain had his way, he would surely choose Ronan to court his daughter. The fact that Brenna desired to be courted by the young warrior would also be taken into account. None of this was of his concern unless, of course, it somehow caused Caolyn to be held in disfavor or worse to be banished from the village. This thought only made Drest more committed to the task of learning more about Ronan.

As Drest was about to mount his horse, the Chieftain's noticed him. "Ho, Drest, my friend, what brings you here so early on this day? I am about to be off to a hunt. Would it be in your favor to join me?"

"No, kind Sir, but thank you for letting me use this horse."

"It is my pleasure,"

"I am about to take my leave of the village for two days. I have friends in the East. I would like to see if they have been blessed with long years as I have. It has been many turnings of the years since we have seen each other." Drest knew that he was not being entirely truthful, but he did not want the Chieftain to think that he was spying on Ronan. It would be Drest who would lose favor in that battle.

"Of course, but I fear that you should not travel alone. I do not wish to make you feel you are unable to protect yourself, but you are of advanced years. May I send one of the warriors to accompany you?"

"Thank you, Sir, could you spare Aedan?"

"A good choice, Drest.

"Thank you Chieftain, I do not see us away longer than two sunsets. The road is a good one to the East, and if my friends no longer walk this ground, I shall be back in quick time."

"Aye, then, may the gods be with you. I shall tell the Head of the Guard that Aedan is to be ready to ride as soon as you get to the stable."

"Many thanks and may Nodens bless your dogs and the hunt. May you return with a full sack!" Drest responded as he waved the Chieftain off.

"Hmm, it will be good to have Aedan and his young eyes and ears along for the company. I must be careful to keep safe the true reason for the trip. I do not want Aedan to think that I do not see Ronan in a good light but, I must also satisfy the feeling gnawing at my gut that there is something about his past that is not right."

Drest went back to his sleeping quarters for a few things for the journey and then to the stables to find Aedan.

XXIV

When Drest arrived at the stables, he found Aedan saddling his mount and preparing to ride. "Ho, Aedan, I trust you are preparing to ride with me on this fine day!"

"Aye, Sir Drest, I have received a request from the Captain of the Guard. He has advised that you are looking to visit friends to the east of the village and you would like some company. I am happy to travel with you. The journey will relieve me of night guard duty as well as provide me with the joy of good company."

"You are too kind my young lad. The Chieftain feels at my age I should have someone to protect me on a short journey. Do not get old, my son. The young forget that we were once strong and able bodied. I must say, though, I often forget my years until I am nearly falling asleep at a task. It will be good to have the company, and perhaps we can speak of what lessons life has given me, and you can learn from my mistakes."

Drest picked out a horse, asking the stable boy, "So, young master, is this a good and faithful ride for an old warrior?"

"Tis sir, he will not tire easily and he is gentle. He can also go with great speed if needed," the young boy replied.

"Then make the steed ready and Aedan and I will be off. And here is a bit of fresh bread and a sweet from the kitchen for your troubles."

"Thank you, sir. It seems I am always hungry and often do not have time to eat fully."

Drest patted the young boy on the back as he prepared to mount. "If the journey is a good one, I will bring you back something good from the East, perhaps a small pheasant for you to have for your own? You must eat, Lad, you are a growing boy."

The two riders were off to the East -- Drest to gather information and Aedan to be his aide if needed. "If it pleases you, Gods, may I learn more about this young Ronan so that my heart and mind can rest easy," Drest offered a prayer as they set off.

XXV

The small group of travelers moving west to set the wish right had stopped for a mid- day rest and to eat a light meal. Things were being gathered to finish the journey to Nora's family home. It was still a beautiful day and, if all went well, they should be at Nora's kin's well before the sun was half way to the horizon.

Caolyn was busy gathering up the last of the eating tools and cups when Cynara approached. "Caolyn, when we reach Nora's kin and all the pleasantries have been put away, I will need to spend time with you doing some preparation for the wishing ceremony."

"Of course, Auntie, I have been thinking heavily upon the task and remembering the mistakes that I made when casting the first wish. I believe I have learned much from my error."

"Good, good, Caolyn, but that is not enough. We must be sure that you have the words correct and we must be sure to use the proper herbs. We must also be alert to the weather and the moon rise. This will be helpful in guiding the ceremonial smoke to Caolainn, the Goddess of wishes, your namesake. You will have but one chance to get this right. I am told that the wishing stone is quite large. You will have to be strong in mind, body and spirit in order to get the stone carrying the wish to be tossed over the peak. In addition, you will have to toss it with your back toward the large stone. Your mind will have to be clear of everything except for the sight of the stone in your mind's eye. Do you understand?"

Caolyn knew that her auntie was as concerned for her as she was for herself. If her auntie only knew how fitful her sleep had been and what strange dreams she had had about all of this wishing. Calming her sleep with crushed lavender on her pillow and drinking lavender tea did not seem to help. She knew she must have Cynara's faith and trust to make everything right.

"I do understand, Auntie, and I have been praying to the Goddess, rehearsing in my mind the words I must say when making the wish. I am also aware that we cannot be too long in the place of the wishing stone as some stories have come back that it is a cursed place ever since the giant was buried by Arawen's anger. I will do my best."

"Good, my young maid," Cynara responded. Cynara was thinking how much Caolyn had matured since that night at her home more than two moons past. The girl was becoming the woman she was called to be. "You would be proud of this daughter, Myra," she thought.

Ronan broke the mood when he approached the two women stating, "Are we prepared to be off my Ladies?"

"Indeed, dear, Sir," Cynara replied. "How much longer will the journey be?"

"I am judging by the sun that we should see Nora's roof top before the sun sinks low in the sky." Of course, that is if we encounter empty roads and good weather the rest of the way."

"Thank you Sir. This has been a most easy journey thus far. May the gods continue to bless us." Cynara turned went to the wagon, and they began the final piece of the journey to Nora's kin.

The time on the road was uneventful. The afternoon passed pleasantly for the little group. Brian and Nora were chatting away on the wagon seat, enjoying each other's company. Cynara was dozing in the back of the wagon with the afternoon sun pleasantly warming her face and old bones. As for Ronan and Caolyn, they too were enjoying the peaceful ride side by side.

Suddenly Nora called. "I believe we will see the thatched roof of my family home around the next bend, Sir Ronan!"

"Aye, Mistress Nora, I shall be on the watch." The words were no sooner spoken when Nora called again.

"There, Brian, stand up. I can see smoke rising from the roof top! I am nearly home!"

Brian stood up to take a look, and Nora grabbed the reins and gently slapped the mule's backside. "Be off, mule, I am home! I am home!" With that, the wagon lurched forward shaking Cynara awake and nearly knocking Brian off the wagon seat.

Brian laughed and shook his head. "How I wish you could be that happy to see me, Nora!"

Nora paid no attention and, in a moment, was riding past Ronan and Caolyn. "It would seem that the trip has been a good one for Nora thus far," Caolyn said with a smile. "Tis good to see her so happy."

"Indeed," Ronan responded. "Let us not be in too great a hurry to catch up to her. She has Brian and Cynara with her, and we will allow them a moment before we set upon them."

"Agreed. There will be time for introductions on our arrival." Ronan reached for Caolyn's hand and tried to pull her a little closer. At that moment, a great wind came up and Ronan's horse reared back. Caolyn looked about but did not see any further sign of impending bad weather.

The wind calmed as quickly as it had risen. Caolyn and Ronan looked at each other with confusion. "What, pray heaven, was that!" Ronan asked.

"I fear I have no answer! I wish Nora was here; perhaps she would have foreseen the strange happening and given us warning. Perhaps it is a sign that we are entering the land of bad legends. I will have to ask Cynara about this after the evening repast."

Ronan and Caolyn continued on to Nora's home. The sweet moment had been broken.

XXVI

By the time Ronan and Caolyn caught up to the group gathered around Nora's home, all of Nora's family had come out to greet the arriving party. Nora's mother was smiling and hugging her so tightly that it seemed she would never let her go. All of the brothers and sisters were dancing around Nora and their mother and singing happy songs. Caolyn could feel the joy rise inside of her; she was very happy for Nora. She felt a pang of regret, knowing that she had never had and might never have this sense of family. Nora was truly blessed.

When Nora's mother had stopped her hugging, she collected herself and stopped to ask pardon of Cynara, Ronan, Caolyn, and of course, Brian. "Please, Everyone, pardon my selfishness in not making proper introductions for you."

"Do not be silly, my dear," Cynara interrupted. "It is easy to feel your joy at the reunion of your family. We are the intruders on this happy day." Cynara walked to Nora's mother and offered her two arms in an open embrace. "I am Cynara of the House of Maidens. Pointing to the rest of the group and waving them closer she continued. "This is Sir Ronan, our leader and protector; this is my niece, Caolyn and our reason for the trip; and lastly, this is Master Brian, our helper and master of many things needed for the journey."

Ronan stepped forward and offered a respectful nod, Caolyn bowed simply and Brian blushed and waved. After a few more pleasantries, Nora's mother curtsied and introduced herself and the children. "I am Margaret, the owner of this home and mother of this brood." Pointing at each child she introduced them. "This is Padraic, the eldest boy at 12 years. Next, are Conan, who is nearly 11; then Maeve, who is 9 and lastly, Mary, who is the baby at 8." The four children bowed and collectively stated "Welcome."

"Come now," Margaret began as she moved toward the small home. "We shall take a small evening meal and set about sleeping arrangements and plans for the purpose of your journey."

As they all walked toward the house, Brian spoke, "Mistress Margaret, if it will be all right, I would like to unhitch the mule and unsaddle the horses and then join you. It has been a long day, and they could use a rest and some freedom."

"Of course, Padraic, show Brian where he can care for the animals and where he can find food and water for them. Now don't be wasting your time, lads. The food is nearly ready."

Padraic walked toward Brian and clapped him on the shoulder. "Come along, Sir. I will help you with the task."

"No need to call me sir," Brian responded. "I am a long way off from that kind of a rank." The two boys went to the open shed where the animals would rest for the night.

XXVII

Drest and Aedan had set off to the East. Their journey would not be long, and they surely would be in the territory known as Cill Dara before sunset. Drest was deep in thought, remembering the last time he had traveled east to the lowlands. He remembered following the track of one of the many rivers, the An Bohinn, and several others, when he had searched for Caolyn's sire in the past. He felt the old sorrow rise in his heart, and he felt the old rush of anger in his spirit. What a waste of a life. His poor sister Myra, full with child and full with the hope that this warrior, once he knew of the child, would come back to her. Little did she or anyone, even Drest himself, think that the man would not be honorable. Drest was shaken back to reality by the sound of Aedan's voice.

"Sir Drest, are you asleep on your mount?"

"Hmm, um, Aedan, forgive me, my son, I have been lost in the past. It happens as one takes on more years. I was thinking about the chances of finding my old warrior friend. He has at least as many years on him as I, perhaps more. 'Tis possible we will not find him, or if we do, he may not be able to converse with me. I hope I have not taken you on a fool's journey."

"Do not concern yourself, Drest, I am happy to be in your company even if you spend it sleeping," Aedan teased. "Let us stop and walk about a bit and have some nourishment. We will still have plenty of time when we arrive at our destination to search for your friend."

"Yes, lad, it will be good to walk a bit and sup. My legs feel as if they lack strength. I fear it is long since I have ridden such a distance."

The two men reined their horses to a halt and slid down from their mounts. They took their food bags to the shade at the side of their road to eat their simple meal.

"The ride is an easy one, Drest. This old warrior friend you speak of, what is he called? Have you fought in battle with him in the past?"

"I fear, Aedan, I have not been completely honest with you. I confess that, in my heart, I still hope to have a reckoning with the man who sired Caolyn. I want him, if alive he may be, to acknowledge that he is her sire. Perhaps, if he has regrets as do I at this age, he may find a way to make amends. I may want too much, but it may be a blessing for him in his old age and for Caolyn to know her father."

As Drest spoke the words, he knew he was still not being honest, for the true reason for the journey was to find out more about Ronan. This he must keep in his own counsel, at least for the time being. It was a bit of luck that Ronan was from the area of Caolyn's sire. He hoped both matters can be settled.

"So, you do not want to find the old warrior friend? Surely, I would understand your wanting to find Caolyn's sire. Do not worry, Drest, I am happy to accompany you and be at your side to assist in any way. If you have had enough rest we should be going."

Aedan smiled as he helped Drest to his feet. He was also thinking that he would be honored to do anything to make Caolyn happy. He was becoming fond of Drest as well.

"You are a good young man, Aedan. Caolyn and Ronan are blessed to call you friend. Let us be back on the road."

XXVIII

As the two men followed the road that ran close to the river, they saw huts come into view. Then they encountered the habitants, who seemed poor and struggling to get along. There was not much in the way of a village as yet, and the people seemed to be doing their best to survive on the land and on what the river could supply.

Aedan suggested they ask if there were a village close by and seek directions so they might inquire about the man Drest was seeking. Drest agreed, and Aedan rode his horse closer to the river to address a young man fishing on the shore.

"Ho, young sir, I am Aedan, a warrior from the West seeking your closest village. Can you offer help?"

The young man turned and smiled at Aedan. "Aye, Sir, if you but travel a small distance there is a gathering of huts. It is where the river slows and flows into an inlet. It is small and hardly a village, but is a widow there assists travelers and makes a fine ale. Perhaps she can provide some comfort from your travels."

Aedan thanked the boy and tossed him a coin for his troubles. The boy look surprised and Aedan knew that he most likely had never had that much coin for himself.

The boy bowed low and said a hardy "Bless you, kind sir!" Aedan waved and trotted back to Drest with the news that they were not far from a "village," where they might find some information and a pint of ale. The two men continued on.

It wasn't long before smoke could be seen rising above the trees. "Ho, Aedan, look east. I believe that rising smoke may be from the tiny village. It is getting near the time that hearth fires begin to cook the evening meal. We must be close," Drest announced.

"Indeed, Drest, we shall soon take our leave from this day of riding. We shall seek out the widow the lad at the river mentioned and attempt to secure food and lodging for the night."

"My young Aedan, my backside is singing your praises," Drest said with a chuckle. "I have forgotten what it feels like to be long in the saddle. A bit of hot food and a sip of ale will be a treasure."

Aedan laughed along with Drest as he thought that the old warrior had not fared too badly. They only needed to stop once on the road and the trip offered a decent weather day.

The two rounded the bend, which opened to a small grove of trees where a circle of several tidy huts stood back from the river. The ground was nestled on a tiny inlet and provided a gentle slope to the river. It was a peaceful and simple view to take in.

There were several children playing on the shore, and a few women tending gardens or fishing. It was not long before word passed around that two strangers had entered their humble surroundings. Soon, a young fellow, who appeared slightly younger than Aedan, approached the men. "Ho strangers, what brings you here to our humble baile? I am Owen, son of the Master of this baile."

"Ho, Owen. I am Drest, and I come from near great Lake Corrib. This is my young friend Aedan. He serves the Chieftain who protects the village that is near the House of Maidens. We are here searching for an old warrior friend of mine; I pray to the gods he may still be alive."

"The House of Maidens is well known even here in this small place," Owen responded. "Come, walk among us; we are happy to provide you with company and assist you as best we can with finding your old friend. It should not be difficult for there are not many among us that are as old as you are dear Sir."

Aedan slid down from his mount and assisted Drest. He then walked toward the young man with a smile and extended arm. "Be careful who you address as 'old'," Aedan chuckled. "He may be long in years but he still considers himself quite adept!"

Owen blushed a little and looked toward Drest. "I meant no disrespect, Sir."

"There is none taken, lad," Drest began. "We were told that there might be a place to find shelter for the night and perhaps have a bit of food and ale. Do you know of a place, Owen?"

"That would be the Widow Finn's, Sir. She has the finest ale about, and since she is now alone, she often takes in travelers for a small price. Her stead is the last hut at the end of this road. You cannot miss it, for if you pass it there is nothing beyond for quite a ride."

"Good lad, we will walk to the hut. My bones speak to me after being so long in the saddle," Drest replied. Drest turned towards Aedan and asked. "What say you,

Aedan? Shall we walk the last bit? I can use the time to stretch my weary bones."

"Let us be off Drest. It will be good for the horses, and I can stretch my legs as well." Turning towards Owen, Aedan thanked him and said, "If you are about after you sup, I would like to ask you about the area here and inquire about Drest's friend. Perhaps you could be of help. There is a cup of ale in it for you as well."

"Thank you, Sir, a cup of ale and finding out news from other parts of the land are always welcome. We see few visitors here from other parts of the country. I will come by before the sun sets." The two men turned and walked towards the direction of the widow's home.

It was only a matter of moments before they came upon a large hut that appeared to be the last one in the baile. Outside of the place was a thatched covering attached to the hut where a horse and mule were already tethered to posts and hay and a water trough was there for the animals. There was a lad not yet fully grown who was minding the horses and he looked up as Drest and Aedan approached.

"Ho, Lad," Aedan began. "Might this be the home of the Widow Finn, who provides a place to sleep and a meal for travelers?"

"Indeed, Sir. For a few pence the widow will provide a clean bed and shelter for the horses. A meal and ale can be paid for also, in her keeping room, which is open to travelers and local folk. I am the widow's brother's son, Mac. I am happy to assist you."

"Many thanks, Mac," Aedan responded. We will be needing two beds for this night and two fine cups of ale. This is Sir Drest, my traveling companion and friend."

"Drest will be fine, Mac. No need for formalities

here. We are pleased to have found a place for a night's rest. I fear I am too old for ground sleeping any longer. The addition of ale and nourishment is also a blessing."

"Come along then, Sirs, I will bring you to my aunt, the widow, who owns this place, and we will get you settled. Then, I will be about the care of your horses."

The men went along to the house. Once inside, they found a warm peat fire in the hearth and a large pot on the fire, giving off a wonderful smell. A tiny woman was stirring the pot from which emanated the aroma of a hearty stew.

"Aunt Brigid, we have two men seeking a bed for the night and something to fill their bellies and quench their thirst," Mac said.

The tiny women turned toward the group and her warm smile was as inviting as the rest of the environment. "Come in, come in. I am Brigid Finn. I see you have met Mac, and I trust he has explained the fare and arrangements to you. I am most pleased to have you here."

Aedan and Drest both nodded toward Brigid. "We are pleased to have found your place," Drest began. "We will be with you for this one night. Can you show us where we will sleep and where we might shake off some of the dust of the road?"

"Come along, I have a room that Mac has added on to our hut. It has space for both of you and it should be quiet and restful. You may go out through the back and to the river if you wish to freshen yourself from the travels, but tarry. Mac has a fine appetite, and I want to be sure you have your fill before he attacks the food," Brigid said with a chuckle.

The men followed Brigid to the back and found the

room to be more than adequate. Brigid excused herself and returned to the hearth to finish the meal preparations.

Once outside, Drest and Aedan removed their heavy riding capes and clothing and both dunked their heads into the river. "Aedan, perhaps while we sup we can inquire about the warrior that was Caolyn's sire. Brigid or Mac may know of him or someone my age that lives about."

"Yes, I think that we should inquire as soon as we are able. I am hoping that if he is somewhere near that we will find him this night or early in the morn. If the gods are with us, we can start back to our village early in the day."

"Yes, yes, that would be good. Come let us go and enjoy our stew and have some of the fine ale we have heard about."

The two companions went back to the hut and prepared for their meal and what they hoped would be an evening of discovery of the whereabouts of an old warrior.

XXIX

When Aedan and Drest entered the main room in the homestead, there were already several others milling about with cups of ale in their hands. They all seemed to be locals who knew each other. Mistress Brigid came over to the two travelers with a pleasant smile on her face. "Come along, Sirs. Would you be ready to sup, or are you here to just quench your thirst. There is a fine lamb stew in the pot and I have baked fresh bread."

"I believe we need to fill our bellies and quench our thirst, Mistress," Aedan responded as he looked toward Drest, who nodded in agreement. "We have heard much about your fine ale from the many folk along the river."

Brigid laughed, "When there is almost no ale in the close whereabouts it is no task to be fine. I shall bring you both the ale and the lamb stew. It is simple fare but it will satisfy you as well."

Brigid made her way to the hearth while the two set about finding a spot to share not far from the warmth of fire. Several men were also eating at the long table.

They were barely seated when one of the men bid them welcome. The conversation soon turned to the usual questions of where they were from, and what had brought them to, in their words, "this spit of a place."

Drest introduced himself first and told taking this journey to find an old warrior friend, pondering if he still might be alive. He explained that Aedan was his travel companion and there to be of assistance. The men around the table listened to the story of the two strangers. Once Aedan and Drest had finished speaking, one of the men reached his hand across the table to Drest and began to speak.

"I am Bart, a farmer from this land. There are few old warriors such as yourself about any longer. There may be one, though that you can speak with, though he be a mean- spirited old man." Drest and Aedan reached across the table and shook the farmer's hand.

"What can you tell us of this man?" Drest inquired.

"He is long in years, such as yourself. He lives alone in what cannot be called a home. He is mean in manner and speech, and he has little or no company. T'is said he beat his woman after his son left. T'is said the young lad could not stand to be around him. There was a daughter that died from a fever and another daughter not quite grown to womanhood yet. She is somewhere around this area."

Another man at the table interrupted. "Tis true. His daughter is Fiona. She has fostered herself to a widow who has three small bairns. She helps mind the little ones and tends the sheep for a place to sleep and food. She could no longer stand to be around her sire. The man was beastly towards her. When she found her way to the widow's after a bad row with her da, she was half starved and filthy."

Drest listened intently and his thoughts were that they had possibly described the man he sought. If he would not do right by his own child, he most certainly would not even offer to recognize Caolyn as his own.

"How can we find the lass Fiona?" Drest asked. "Perhaps she can bring us to her sire if we offer protection to her."

As the men were discussing information about the girl named Fiona and her sire, the door to the keeping room opened. Owen, the young man, who had given them assistance and directions, entered the room.

"Ho, Owen," Aedan greeted him. "Come, that ale I promised is here for you."

As Owen walked toward the group, the other men greeted him warmly. He sat and Brigid brought him his ale. The discussion soon turned back to Fiona. Bart told them that Fiona, often brought her da a basket of food, but usually left it near the gate.

Owen interrupted to say that the widow's home was only a short ride on the main road. "Perhaps you could go in the morn. You should know that Fiona's da is an evil man. He lives on ale and scrounges for food. Fiona goes rarely to his hut since the widow rescued her."

"What do you mean rescued?" Drest inquired.

"Her da went after her one sunset, and instead of the usual beatings, he was after her for more than a father should be." Owen's face was crimson as he related the story. "The widow's husband was alive then and he gave Fiona's da a thrashing. She was in a bad way and he took her to his wife, who nursed her back to health. The widow refused to let Fiona go back to her da. Soon everyone in the baile had heard of what he had done and what he had in his mind to do to his own child. The men in the village made a pact that they would all be her protector."

As Drest listened to Owen's story he could feel bitterness in his soul. "It would not surprise me if this were not the same man that left Myra. I could feel his putridness even then. Gods help me! If this be he, he will feel my wrath for what he did to my sister and to his own kin and bairn. I feel I will use every last ounce of my life's strength to avenge them all!"

"Drest, you appear ill," Aedan's voice broke into Drest's thoughts.

"Aye, Aedan, to hear a story of such evil and treachery committed towards one's child is disturbing. That is not a man; that is a vile monster."

Resounding "ayes" came from the men seated around the table.

"Perhaps your inquiry about this man should begin at the widow's farmstead," Owen said. "If Fiona is not there, you might find her on the road to her da's with her food basket."

"She must be remarkable, young lass if she holds no anger against her sire, who nearly caused her permanent harm," Drest continued.

"She never gets very close to the hut. She leaves the basket and goes. She has repeated many times that she blames his love of ale for his life's misfortunes and for his manner. She has often been heard saying, "*He is still me da.*"

Drest shook his head, and then he rose and excused himself from the group. "I fear this story has disturbed me to my very soul. I am off to my cot to try to get some much needed sleep. Aedan, no need to come; stay with the lads and enjoy their company. I will see you in the morn."

The men bid Drest a good night. As he walked to his chamber his mind was swirling with thoughts of how he would deal with the man if indeed he was Caolyn's father. He remembered that he forgotten to ask by what name this man was called. He would never forget it, Bain, the one who caused his sister such heartache. He swore by all that was holy that if this were, he there would be a reckoning--by the gods there would be!

XXX

Drest stretched out on his cot and could see the beginning of the sunrise as he turned toward the small window in the room. Aedan was still sleeping soundly with his gentle snoring filling the space. "He must have taken his share of ale to still be slumbering so deeply," Drest thought. "I will do my best to give him a bit more time."

Drest quietly got up from the cot and stole out of the chamber to go to the river and freshen himself. Once outside he could hear busyness in the keeping room and could smell a sweet aroma was rising from the hearth fire. He suddenly felt hungry and thought he would go to the keeping room, once he finished at the river. "Perhaps Brigid will let me break fast early and then Aedan can sleep without my disturbing him."

Once Drest had freshened himself and put on his riding tunic, he walked toward the keeping room. He knocked on the outside door, and in a moment Brigid was there. "Good morning, Sir Drest. I trust you slept well?" Brigid inquired with a pleasant smile.

"Aye, Mistress, your pleasant surroundings and the comfort of a cot rather than the ground made for a restful night. I was wondering if I might have a bit to eat this early in the morn. Aedan is still lost in the dream world, and he deserves a rest after putting up with the likes of an old one like myself."

"You are more than welcome to sup early, Sir. The porridge with berries and sweet cream will be ready soon. I have little to do this early, except to have food ready for the travelers. 'Tis only you and Sir Aedan that have spent this night. Would you prefer ale or mead with your porridge? "

"Mead would be fine and the porridge already smells wonderful, Mistress."

"Come along then, follow me into the keeping room and I will serve you soon." Brigid walked briskly toward the house. "You may have to put up with my prattle and questions as you wait for your meal. 'Tis not often I have a traveler to myself and I enjoy stories that strangers have to share."

"A small price for a good meal and, at my age, I have more stories than you may want to hear," Drest said with a chuckle.

Once inside, Drest made himself comfortable and Brigid set about getting the meal ready for him. "The lads were here long past the time I went to my cot," Brigid started. "They all seemed to get along well and were respectful of my space. Mac would keep the lads in line if need be." Drest noticed how quickly and with much spirit Brigid went about her tasks. She looked to be content with her life's lot.

Once the food was served, Brigid came in with a mug of steaming liquid and sat with Drest at the long table. "So, you are searching for an old warrior friend?" Brigid began.

"Aye, but truth be told I am searching for the sire of

my niece. He is no friend! I want to have a reckoning with this man. He was a warrior as was I, and he helped defend the House of Maidens in a great battle in a time past. He would not do his duty with regards to support for his child. My sister Myra had enjoyed a time with him at a Beltane, and she found herself with child. She asked that I go to the eastern country to find him and tell him of the child. When I found him, he was already promised with another. Together, they had a young boy child and a babe that was crawling about; his wife was also heavy with the coming of another. I tried reasoning with the man, but he forced me away. I did not wish to bring harm to his family."

"When I returned to the House, I spoke of the circumstance with Myra. She begged me to let it be, as she wished no harm to him and the family. It was not long after that when another battle occurred. Once again, the House needed to be defended as well as the village. Our scouts had seen enemies on the march, so warriors were called to make haste to defend, first the village and then the House. That is when this warrior, Bain, returned to defend the village. I prayed that he be killed in battle, but instead, Myra was wounded. This caused the birth of her child to come shortly after. She went on to the other world and the babe was raised in the House."

Brigid could see by Drest's face that even now after so many years, this story cut through to his soul. "Sir Drest, the ways of men are often difficult to understand. One hopes for a good man, and there are many, but there are also those who take advantage of their station. Even a common man is held above the level of a woman. We have very little voice. Your niece was blessed to have you and the House to be raised in, another lass would have been sold off to anyone with the price to pay."

"Thank you. Brigid. I fear I have not been the best relation for my niece, but that is another story. I am here to finally seek justice if her sire is still alive. Do you know of this man we are to visit?'

"I only know the story that you heard last eve. I came here wedded from another village, and my husband drowned in the flooding of the river one spring. I never had any babes of my own, and his sister lives here as well. Mac is her son and he helps me with the travelers. I wish you well with this meeting and hope you will find a way to put your mind at rest."

As Brigid stood up to take her leave Aedan came through the keeping room door.

"Aye, Aedan, the cock has crowed long ago. I thought warriors rose early," Brigid said with a laugh.

Drest turned and greeted Aedan. "My apologies Drest, I fear being away from the village and my duties has caused me to forget my tasks."

"No need for apologies lad; we have ample time to be about our task. Take some of Brigid's wonderful porridge into your belly, and perhaps you might prefer a bit of nettle tea to easy your aching head," Drest said with a twist of a smile on his face.

"Porridge and tea should be the fare for this morn. I trust you have been in my place before?"

"Aye lad, but the wisdom of my years has taught me to be careful when it comes to a night of partaking ale." Both men had a good laugh as Brigid brought Aedan's food and a huge cup of steaming nettle tea to the table.

Aedan did not waste time finishing his meal. Already he could feel the nettle tea easing his aching head. As he stood to leave, and counted out the coins to settle with Brigid, Mac entered the room.

"Ho Mac, I bid you good morn. I was about to fetch you to ready the horses. My late rising has delayed our start. A warrior does not often have time away from his duties and being with new friends made for a good eve."

"I, too, was late to my tasks. My aunt came to my sleeping cot and shook me awake. She does not anger easily, and she knows that I do not often have time for myself. How is your head? Are you affected by the ale?" Mac teased.

"Your aunt's strong nettle tea has eased the pounding. And you, you drank your fair share as well?"

"I am fine. Your mounts are ready and the journey to where Fiona's da lives is short. It would be good if you saw her on the road. She could give you fair warning about her da if need be."

While the two young men were speaking, Drest rose from the table to bid farewell to Brigid. "Are you ready, Sir Aedan, or do you need more nettle?"

"No, Drest, let us go and get this task done, and if time allows, we may be on the return to our village by midday."

Drest turned to Mac and asked. "Might you know the name of Fiona's da? Brigid did not know the name. It would be a great help to be able to address him when we get to his hut."

"His name is Bain. It is said that......" Mac had barely spoken the name when Drest suddenly teetered and grabbed the table for strength. "BAIN! BAIN!" he screamed and then collapsed.

Aedan and Mac caught him before he hit the floor. Brigid ran into the room, "God of gods, what has happened!"

The young men slowly eased Drest to the floor as Brigid ran to them carrying a mug of ale.

"Drest," Aedan began. "Here, take a swallow. Are you ill?"

Drest opened his eyes to take a sip of ale. His color slowly returned to his face. "Bain is the name of Caolyn's sire. It is he! Fiona must be the child that was yet in her mother's womb. There was also a babe crawling about. The wife, where is she? She was heavy with child when I last was here. We must be on our way Aedan; I will have my day of reckoning!" Drest was fighting to sit up and be on his way.

"Sir Drest," Brigid began, "Sit, finish your ale. You shall have your say, but you must be fit to ride. Waiting another few moments will not change the reckoning."

Drest finished his ale, and after several moments seemed to be himself again. He and Aedan made their way to the horses. Mac helped Drest to his mount and Aedan was soon in the saddle as well. Brigid handed Drest a wineskin. "There is mead to use if you feel it necessary. Be safe, my friends."

Both men turned to leave after giving thanks to Mac and Brigid for their kindness. They promised to return with news if the time allowed.

On the short ride to the hut where Bain lived, Drest expressed some confusion with regards to his memory of the first meeting.

"If my mind is not too befuddled with age, Aedan, I thought there were two young ones and the wife was close to the birthing of another. Where are those other children, most likely grown at this time?"

"Certainly Fiona is one of the children. The others may now be grown and moved on, or they may have gone to the other world as well. 'Tis true. Perhaps Fiona can settle the happenings for us. Look, there is the hut. As was told by the men last eve, it is a hovel at best, and I can smell an unclean stench even at this distance."

The place the two men came upon could scarcely be called a hut. The thatched roof was laid open in several places. A thin underfed cat was washing itself while a dog lay listlessly in the dirt. As they got closer, they could see a young maid just leaving a basket by the gate. She turned and looked at the two strangers approaching.

"Ho, Sirs, good morn to ye, I am Fiona, daughter of Bain. I am leaving him provisions. Me da, is not a well man. Life and the drink have not been kind to him."

"Good morn, Mistress Fiona," Aedan began. "I have come with my friend Drest. We are seeking Bain because my friend believes they fought in a great battle together in years past. He was hoping to speak again with him."

Drest studied Fiona. He noticed that there was some resemblance to Caolyn in the girl, though Fiona had light hair and Caolyn's was red as flame. The resemblance lay in their facial features. Fiona had deep blue eyes like Caolyn's, and the lines of their jaws and chins showed a distinct connection to each other. Drest held his counsel for the moment, happy to let Aedan speak for them. He was still shaking from hearing that this was the man who had broken his sister's spirit.

"If your da be ill, Mistress, why do you not bring the basket to his door?" Aedan inquired.

Fiona need not speak; her frightened face told the story of what the men had heard last eve. "B.. b.., I fear me da! He has come at me with sticks and axe and in ways not fit for a father!" Fiona was now shaking and crying at the same time.

Drest slid from his horse and went to the girl. "I am sorry and angered for what you have endured, Mistress. I am Drest, and I have come to seek your sire. We have not been entirely truthful, as your sire is not my friend, but one who caused pain and sorrow to my family. I have come to reckon with him for his past errors. I have no wish to cause you fear or discomfort. Aedan and I will be here to protect you. How might we get your sire to come from the hut?"

"He is rarely out of the shelter, Sir. When I bring provisions, I search from a distance to be sure he is not about, and then, if I do not see him, I may leave the basket inside the gate. Most often, though, I leave the basket here and quickly take my leave."

"Do you think if we hail him by name he would come out?" Aedan now inquired.

"He trusts no one so, of that I cannot be sure."

Drest and Aedan discussed attempting to call Bain from the hut. Drest decided to step inside the gate while Aedan would circle around toward the side of the hut, giving him an advantage should Bain go on the attack. Fiona would mind the horses and stay safely outside the gate.

Once Aedan was positioned, Drest called out to Bain. "Sir Bain, come forth. It is an old warrior who fought with you. I have come to bid you well."

Aedan could see Fiona pacing outside the gate. He was also amazed at the resemblance she had to Caolyn. It wasn't long before Aedan could hear rustling in the hut. A stooped, old man with long dirty hair and overgrown beard emerged from the hut. There was no resemblance to a warrior left in this broken human.

"Who comes to my door? There be no old warrior

friends of mine left. You must be a liar!" Bain screamed as he spat on the ground.

Drest edged closer and kept his eyes on the man who had caused so much misery in his life. "It is I, Drest, brother of Myra and uncle to Caolyn, who you did not have the decency to recognize as the babe you sired. Myra died heartbroken after the birth. I came for vengeance and justice then, but Myra did not wish harm and brokenness on your family. It was at her wish that I let it be."

Bain straightened himself. It was easy to see that he remembered Drest. "What have you come for now? Revenge, money, land for the brat that I fathered? Well, you can have all this for her because my unworthy brats have all left me!" Bain was raving and laughing all at once. He seemed a man possessed.

Drest moved closer. "My hope was that perhaps in your aging you may have seen fit to at least recognize Caolyn as your own. I see now this would be a grave mistake. I have met Fiona. I have heard the stories of your treatment of her, and yet she comes to bid you well."

"Bid me well? That brat will not stay and care for me. She has left me to fend for myself. It is a daughter's duty to care for her father, no matter the circumstance."

Fiona stepped inside the gate and called, "Da, I tried to care for you. You beat and starved me. Then, you made an advance toward me that I could not take. I am your daughter not a mate or wife. The drink has taken your mind!"

Bain looked toward Fiona as he moved toward her, "You belong to me! I will not let you go and now I have help to keep you here."

Drest stepped in front of Bain and Aedan moved

toward them both. Drest raised his arms to stop Bain but Bain pushed him aside. Drest stumbled but did not fall. He stuck out his foot and Bain tripped, falling to the ground. Drest was on him in a heartbeat, punching and hitting with all the might his aged body would allow.

Fiona screamed for it to stop. Aedan went to the two old warriors and pulled them apart. "Enough!" Aedan yelled. "Drest, you have had your revenge. As for you, Bain, stay away from your daughter, or you will answer to me!"

Drest and Bain stood up. It was clear that Drest had gotten the better part of the skirmish. Fiona had come with a bucket of water to offer both men. She would not get close enough to her father to offer the water.

Bain, still red with anger glared at Fiona, "Go, leave me for good, just like your ungrateful brother Ronan! Leaving to serve the Chieftain and leaving his sire to fend for himself. Ungrateful brats, the lot of you!"

Aedan could not believe what he had heard and was about to question Bain when Drest spoke. "Ronan, you have a son Ronan! The great swimmer, the one who aids the Chieftain in the village near the House of Maidens!"

"Yes," Fiona interrupted. "Ronan is my brother, his son. He left a few years back when he could no longer tolerate being with our d a. He comes from time to time and brings me coin to help pay for Da's food and to check on my needs. He was here when I last left. He wanted to come and make Da pay for what he had done to me. I wouldn't have it. I was fine. I just wanted to be left alone and kept safe."

Drest and Aedan looked at each other in shock. They had no need to speak in front of Fiona, but it was clear to each of them what needed to be done next.

Drest turned to Bain, "I had hate in my heart for all you have caused, but what you have done to your own family is far worse than what Myra, Caolyn and I have had to endure. It has been a blessing from the gods that my sister and niece have not had you in their lives. I know your son. He is a fine warrior and a man of honor. He must have learned that from his ma. I will leave you here, living in the misery that comes from a dead and blackened soul. You have earned what your ill deeds have reaped."

Bain sneered as the party of three turned to leave. As they approached the horses Aedan asked Fiona if she would like a ride back to her home with the widow. She consented. It had been an exhausting morning.

XXXI

A edan lifted Fiona onto his horse. She was now sobbing and appeared to be like a frightened rabbit. Drest's heart was aching for the poor lass, who had no real understanding of her circumstance, and for the physical suffering she had already endured. Aedan looked toward Drest. "Perhaps we best move slowly. I will walk alongside the horse while Fiona collects herself." He then lowered his voice, "Drest, can what we heard be true? Can it be possible that Ronan is Caolyn's half-brother, her blood relative!"

"By the account we have heard it would seem to be truth. By the gods, that man has caused more harm than he knows or even could give a care to see!"

"We must tell Fiona the truth and we must make haste to get back to the village. We must make this known to the Lady Ava. Caolyn cannot be hand fasted to Ronan!"

"To be sure, Aedan, but we are at the least a half day's ride from the village, and we have no knowledge of Cynara and Caolyn's success or failure on their journey to the land west."

"I will think on a plan, Drest, but our first concern is to advise Fiona of this news."

"Aye, Lad, may the gods guide our hearts and words in this task."

As they traveled on Fiona seemed to recover herself. "Sir Aedan, I beg your pardon for the actions of me da. It is said that he was not always so mean and spiteful. I barely remember me ma. She and my older sister died when a fever went through the land in years past. Ronan tried to stay and help our sire, but they were always at each other. As soon as I was able to fend for myself, he took his leave and went to join your Chieftain's warriors. He came back as often as he could but…."

"Fiona, you do not have to make excuses for your sire. What he has become may be his own doings or the fate put upon him by the gods. We will be sure that you are safe. Does Ronan know of the recent events that have caused you to be fostered to another home?"

"No, sir, he has not been back for some time. The last time he was with our da, I thought he would kill him. We had no food and the hut was falling down. Ronan fixed the hut then and left money with me, but once he was gone, me da took it for drink."

Drest made Aedan stop and he dismounted. "Fiona, we must speak with you about Ronan."

"Ronan? You know my brother? You have seen him?"

Aedan helped Fiona down from the horse and Drest went to her. "Aye, Lass, Aedan and your brother are friends. They have faced battle together. I, too, fought for our village and the House of Maidens in time past. Come, let us sit while I explain some things that will affect you and perhaps your future."

The three moved toward a grove of trees and sat down. Drest made a silent prayer to the gods and to his sister Myra. "Please guide my words. Let me not hurt this young maid any further. Make my words gentle."

"Many years past," Drest began, "my sister Myra and your da were at the festival of Beltane. There were celebrations and dancing and the two took a liking to each other. They celebrated the feast, as all young ones do, and my sister was found to be with child one moon after the feast. Bain, your da, did not live in the village."

Drest paused and bent his head, trying not to let his anger and sorrow get the best of him. After a moment he began again. "My sister Myra asked if I would try to find his village. She wanted him to know he was going to be a father. She was sure he loved her as much as she loved him. I came to this place and found him. He was with your ma, and two young bairns. Your ma was big with child; this must have been you. I tried to reason with your da. He mocked me and sent me on my way. I wanted revenge for my sister, but I would not take it in front of his family."

By now Drest's voice was beginning to crack. Fiona reached out and touched his arm. "Are you saying that I have another sister? Another sister? One that I can share the things of my heart, soul and thoughts with?"

"Aye, child, but there is also a cloud over this. Ronan does not know that his sister is my niece. He is in love with her and desires to court her. He plans to be hand fasted to Caolyn. She is Ronan and your half-sister."

Fiona jumped to her feet. "We cannot tarry. We must go! I will come away with you. The widow will let me be free of my fostering. I have a sister!"

Fiona could not contain herself; Drest was exhausted from the storytelling. Aedan broke the moment. "Come then, we will go to the widow. Fiona, you must hurry if you wish to come with us. We cannot delay. We must get back to the village before the sun sets on this day."

Aedan lifted Fiona onto the horse and swung himself up as well. Drest mounted his steed and they were off.

XXXII

Meanwhile, back in the land of Iar Connaught, the small group of travelers had settled in with Nora's family. Once the meal had been eaten and the young children bedded down for the night, the group sat with Nora's mother, Margaret, to ask questions about the area near the wishing stone.

"Margaret," Cynara began. "Tell us all you know of the land near the wishing stone. We have been told that the stone is very large in height and that it is often difficult to toss stones taken from the lake over the top when making a wish. We have also been told of the great battle when Arawen punished the giant for pillaging the people in the land there. We know the stories, but we must know of the truth in them and of any other dangers."

"Aye, Cynara, there is much legend and truth mixed into the stories. I will tell you all I know. It is said, the safest time to go is when the sun is highest in the sky. At that time there is little shadow that can fall on the stone and the Giant's hand is clearly visible. Once the sun starts to move past the midday, the land becomes more mysterious. There are stories that the hand often trembles when wishes are made, but I have not heard this directly from any who have passed there."

Everyone was listening intently to the story when suddenly Nora stood up and appeared lost. She was shaking and speaking in a manner unfamiliar to anyone. Caolyn and Brian rushed to assist her.

"STOP!" Cynara said in a strong but barely raised voice. "Nora is seeing something not of this place. Do not disturb the sight. She may be seeing something that will be of help to us."

Nora continued to speak, but no one could understand her. Soon she crumpled to the floor.

"Wait!" Cynara commanded. "Do not waken her. It is better for one to come around in their own time after a vision."

In a few moments Nora was awake and calling for Caolyn. Caolyn went to her side. "I am here, Nora. Are you yourself?"

"I am Caolyn, I have seen what may happen on the morrow. You must take as little time as you are able in this place. Something is afoot. I could see the giant's hand lifting from the ground as you were at the wishing stone. I could hear the god Arawen forcing it back into the ground. For a moment, it seemed as if he would come free and take you. The sky darkened and then Banba, the great goddess of war, appeared with a beautiful lady, who at first appeared to be you, but that cannot be true. The lady said 'Hurry my daughter. Believe! You are able to complete this task, but you must make haste!' Banba then spoke to you saying, 'I will hold back the Giant. He cannot defeat Arawen and me, but my time here is short. You must hurry.' Then, I woke."

Cynara now went to Nora and Caolyn. "Nora, you have had a helpful vision. This will assist us to prepare for tomorrow."

Looking at Caolyn, Cynara began, "Caolyn, the woman with Banba must have been your mother, Myra. A mother's protection can reach beyond the grave. Know that she and Banba will protect you, but we must heed the advice and make haste when we are at the wishing stone. Come now, we prepare!"

The remainder of the night found Cynara and Caolyn preparing to make the wish right and thinking on all that had transpired since the wish was made. By now, Caolyn, had come to terms with the fact that, once the wish was made right, Ronan would most likely be lost to her as a suitor. Brenna desired Ronan and she was the Chieftain's daughter, as well as Caolyn's closest friend. Caolyn was also feeling a bit guilty for not telling Ronan that he was Brenna's desired suitor. "How can I tell Ronan about Brenna's feelings, when he has expressed a desire, to court me? It has been pleasant spending time with him on this journey, though I had too little time alone with him. Strange with all that has been going on, Auntie hearing voices, the wind coming up suddenly whenever Ronan and I seem to have a moment together. And now, Nora's vision. Is my mother, the one who gave me life as she lay dying, protecting me? Will she be with me when I make the wish?"

"Caolyn, Caolyn, come out of your thoughts! We have much to do and settle before this night is over!" Cynara broke the pattern of thoughts that were rushing through Caolyn's mind. "Come, we make our plan."

The two women sat together and Cynara began. "I have sent Brian and Ronan off with Padriac to become familiar with the road we must travel. Padriac knows the road well and will be able point out any places that may be of danger to us. It will be good to have had them travel the road at least once. It may be necessary for us to make haste to escape. I have sent Nora to bed to rest. Her mother has given her a strong tea of chamomile and lavender. I added rose petals for calming and poured a bit of mead into her cup. She must be well rested in the morn. Now tell me what you have prepared."

"Auntie, I have been practicing my concentration and visualizing the stone. I heard Padriac telling Brian that the wishing stone is as high as a full-grown man's arm times ten. I hope that I will have the strength and power to send the stone over the peak. Here is the bay leaf on which I have inscribed Ronan's name and the cord made from a piece of Brenna's garment and hair to bind the leaf to the stone."

As Caolyn was handed the cord and the leaf to Cynara her hand trembled and Cynara looked into her face. "Caolyn, I know this is difficult for you. You hoped to have Ronan for yourself. Things of the heart are always difficult, child, but we must always act for the greater good. When one is committed to the House of Maidens and given special talents, we, the chosen, must always put others before ourselves. You must be strong in this Caolyn." Cynara gently touched Caolyn's cheek and tried to keep her words and tone gentle.

"I understand, Auntie. The Goddess is guiding my fate, and I am committed to her will, but it can still hurt. Sometimes I feel I will never have a family to call my own."

"By the Goddess, Caolyn! You are barely a full-grown woman! There is much time for you to have your heart's desire, though it may be with one other than Ronan. Enough now of this sentiment. We must make a power spell that will help carry the stone you toss over the peak of the wishing stone. We do not have much time before we must settle for the night. In addition, we must make an early start in the morn."

The remainder of the night found Caolyn and Cynara practicing the words they would use during the ceremony of tossing the stone to make the wish right. Ronan, Brian and Padriac returned to the dwelling, having ridden the road to the stone. They went only as far as they dared because of the lateness of the day and the sun setting upon the horizon. Padriac was forceful with his words as he explained that they should not take the chance being near the Wishing stone or the giant's hand as night was falling upon the land.

"Sir Ronan, I have been once to the Stone. It was in full sun light, and still I felt a sense of mystery and danger. Had Nora come on this ride she might have been of help. At least now the road will be somewhat familiar to you."

"Aye, Padriac, tis good that we prepared in this way. Even if Nora had been able to come along, I fear she could not withstand another vision this night. She needs rest for the morrow's task. Brian, what say you about the road and land we must travel?"

Brian had been lost in his thoughts and concerns for Nora. He admitted to himself that he was fearful of her "gift." He was a simple lad and did not understand many of the things that he had seen at the House of Maidens. He was sure of two things--he loved Nora and he trusted the women he served at the House. "Ronan, if this small task of seeing the road before tomorrow's task helps with our duties to our friends, then I am willing to do anything."

"Good lads, let us bed the horses and mull over how we might escape if we need to do so."

After the three young men went to the stables to settle the horses, they planned that, on the morrow, Brian would stay with the wagon that would carry Nora, Cynara and Caolyn. They would try to get as close to the Wishing Stone as possible so that, once the wish was made, Caolyn could hasten to the wagon and be off. They would hitch one of the horses rather than the mule to the wagon and, thus, could escape more quickly. Ronan would be on his mount close to the giant's hand and in a position to grab Caolyn if needed. Padriac would be the eyes of the group scouring for any danger that might be upon them. They would signal with a bird call to alert each other in the event of danger.

With their plans completed they bade each other good night and parted, pledging to be united in their task for the next day.

XXXIII

Ronan could not seem to settle down this night; the fact that Brian and the animals were snoring in deep slumber, did not help. His mind was as anxious as it was on the night before a battle or when he was spying on a ship while he swam near it in order to hear of enemy battle plans.

He had heard the Lady Ava's words, as well as, Cynara's. He understood that he might have a difficult task ahead. If he were being honest with himself, the legend heard this day about the ground trembling at certain times around the giant's hand, along with Nora's vision, left him quite unsettled. Perhaps, the Lady and Cynara were correct regarding their feelings that this would be no easy journey. The group did need a protector. He decided to get up and walk a bit to see if the night air would clear his mind.

Walking about the homestead, he thought of Caolyn, sleeping in the house. Would this business of wishes ever be behind them so he could formally court her? He did not know the whole story of the wish. He knew only of the part where it went wrong and now, as a result, every warrior wanted to court Brenna. Brenna was a beautiful maid and the Chieftain's daughter. It would be of great favor to be taken into the Chieftain's family. "Stop this mind chatter!!" Ronan said to himself. "I must keep my head in the proper frame of thought. It will be good to have this behind me." Ronan made his way back to the barn to sleep, but it would not be a night for a good rest.

When Ronan finally drifted off to sleep, it was a sleep crowded with dreams. He saw himself at the place of the Wishing Stone. He could see Brian at the ready in the wagon, and he could see Cynara and Nora perched on a knoll to the side of the Wishing Stone. He saw Padraic there as well, with his knife drawn for protection. He then saw Caolyn, standing in front of the Stone, holding in her hand a stone from the lough Corrib. She looked so small beside the great stone, but she did not seem afraid.

Next, he saw himself with his hand on the hilt of his sword and his battle helmet covering his head. Caolyn was speaking, but he could not hear her words. Perhaps she was speaking the words of a spell that would make the wish come to pass. Suddenly, the ground began to tremble and the wind came up. He could see himself shouting at Caolyn, warning her to make haste and be done with the task. The ground shaking increased; the sky was darkening and he could see the God Arawen, just as Nora foretold. He then heard what sounded like the crashing of waves, but they were not near the sea. He turned to see lough Corrib churning and the water rising. For the first time in his warrior life, he was afraid and then he woke.

He was shivering and yet his garments were wet with sweat. "Was this a warning of sorts? What did it mean? I must make haste to dress and seek out Cynara," he thought. "Perhaps she can make sense of this dream. I cannot let this cloud my judgement and my good sense. I need my wits about me on this day! May Arawen be my guide and protector?"

XXXIV

Ronan quickly got up from his bed of hay and dressed himself. The sun was barely peeking over the horizon. Brian and the horses were still sleeping. He quietly slipped out of the barn and made his way to the small cottage in search of Cynara. He found her behind the house, and he stopped as she seemed lost in thought. Her eyes were closed, and he could hear her murmuring some sort of chant, though he could not hear the words. Perhaps she was praying to the Goddess, he thought. "We will need much help from the divine beings on this day," he almost said aloud. He took care not to disturb Cynara, but he also wanted to consult her about his dream.

Cynara stopped her chanting and turned toward Ronan. "You are up early, my young Warrior," she began. "Your face gives you away. Are you troubled? did you not sleep?"

"Mistress Cynara, I have had little rest and my sleep was fraught with troubling dreams. I was hoping you could provide me a sense of meaning if I share my dream with you."

"Come, Ronan, we will talk as we break fast. The house is not awake, but I have brought out tea from the hearth kettle and a bit of bread. Let me get another cup for you. I will be quick and quiet."

Cynara went into the house and Ronan found a small bench where Cynara had set her meal. She returned before Ronan could even sit down.

"So, the dream?" Cynara inquired.

Ronan explained everything he had seen in his dream and was soon at the part where lough Corrib was churning. "I don't understand. Even though the lough is large, it is not the sea. I was concerned by the distraction which stole my concentration from the trembling ground and the movement of the hand. Do you think that the giant's hand could cause the lough to have waves? It would seem the distance would be too far. Is it a sign of foreboding? I fear that I may have misunderstood the dangers in this strange part of country. Pray, Mistress, what do you make of this?"

"I feel that your dream may have a connection to Nora's vision. She saw the hand trembling and the ground moving, but she also saw the protection of Arawen and Banba, and Caolyn's mother come to her aid. Perhaps the god of the sea Manannan, called Mac Lir, has taken up a place in the lough to come to your aid, Ronan?"

"I hope, Mistress, that you are correct," Ronan said shaking his head. "Mac Lir is a god of the sea and is called 'wave sweeper' in many legends. I have never sought his protection, but if he is about, I will take it. I cannot wait any longer to have this journey behind us."

"I am with you, Ronan. The sooner we can be done and on our way back to the House, the better for all of us. Go now and ready the wagon and horses and we will be about getting ready for the task at hand. I also have a few ideas to protect us, and I will be ready to use them should the need arise. Caolyn is ready now, she must have the belief in herself, to carry out the task."

The two parted and went their own ways to prepare for the journey to the Wishing Stone. Ronan went back to the stable to find Brian awake, and readying the wagon and the horses. Padriac was also about, offering help to Brian as needed.

"Ho Ronan, we were just speaking of where you might be at such an early hour. Come, see if we have prepared your mount and the wagon to your liking," Brian remarked.

"I have been to seek Cynara's counsel before we begin this journey. My warrior's gut is giving me warnings regarding the task at hand. I hope we have prepared well."

"What troubles you, Sir?" Padriac asked. "Might the vision Nora spoke of be the cause of your concern?"

"Aye, Padriac, that and my own troubled dream in the night past. I am not one that takes much stock in dreams. It goes against my common sense, but the dream I had seemed to have much in common with Nora's vision. Cynara has advised that she is well prepared for any troubles and that Caolyn has prepared herself as well. I pray that this task can be completed with haste, and we can be away from the stone and the mystery that surrounds a place of enchantment and foreboding tales."

"Have no fear, Aedan, Padriac and I will be on the ready. You must have faith that we will assist you," Brian stated.

"Aye, you lads are young and strong, and with the god's blessing, that will be enough," Aedan responded. His thoughts, however, were full of concern that, if things did not go well, he was the only seasoned fighter among the group. He knew the women of the House had talents and abilities that he did not understand. "I have no trouble with trusting myself to another warrior but....." His thoughts trailed off as he fought to bring himself back to the task at hand. "Come, Lads, let us gather the rest of the group and put a finish to this task."

Meanwhile, Cynara had gone back to the house to be sure that Nora and Caolyn were ready for the ride to the Wishing Stone. Margaret had prepared food for the girls to break fast and both were readying themselves for the day.

"Good morn, Mistress Cynara," Margaret greeted. "I have readied the maids for their day."

"Good morn to you as well, Margaret," Cynara returned the greeting and gave a nod of acknowledgement to Caolyn and Nora. "I am pleased to see everyone at the ready. I have a few things to gather for the ride. I have seen Ronan this morn and he has gone to the stable to finish the preparation of the wagon and horses. We should be on our way shortly."

Cynara went to her sleeping cot where she had left her bundle of protective herbs and plants. She had a few tricks up her sleeve, if needed, to assist Ronan in protecting the group.

When Cynara returned to the keeping room, she found Nora and her mother in an embrace. "Be safe, my daughter," Margaret was saying. "I do not understand your gift, but I can also see that you have learned much during your time at the House. I can see that the good women there have done much to teach you how to manage your abilities. I am trusting that, with all on this journey, you are in good hands, but that does not dismiss the fear I have for your safety, as well as that of your companions."

"Ma, I too have fear, but I know I could not be more prepared for this than I am. Cynara has helped me to understand more of my abilities, and Lady Ava has put great trust in me by allowing me to assist in this task. I have good wits, thanks to your teaching, Ma. I am confident that with my gift of fey and the help of my companions, we will see this through."

Margaret's eyes filled up as she hugged Nora closer to her. She turned to Cynara, who was watching the scene. "I have lost babes and my good husband, Cynara. I could not bear to lose my eldest child. It was a great sacrifice to foster her to the House and that was difficult, but if I were to lose her forever……"

Cynara went to Margaret and clasped both her hands. "Margaret, I promise you that we will all do what is necessary to protect the lives of everyone on this journey. I promise you I will protect Nora as I would Caolyn. You have my word."

Cynara and Margaret separated from each other, and it was Nora who broke the moment. "Come, we must not tarry any longer." She ran to Margaret for a final hug and they were off.

XXXV

When Aedan, Drest and Fiona arrived at the widow's home where Fiona was fostered, she quickly went to gather her few possessions while Drest explained the circumstance. The widow was more than pleased that Fiona would be reunited with her brother and would meet her half-sister. "The lass has been a great help here, but she needs to be away from this place. There is always the fear that her miserable sire will come for her and take her away. If you are to make haste you will need another mount. Take the horse that my husband's brother boards here. I will explain the reason for his going."

"Thank you Mistress," Drest responded. He reached into his garments for his pouch where he kept coin. "This is payment for the horse. I cannot guarantee that we will return. You have been most kind." The widow tried to wave off the offer of money, but Drest wouldn't have it.

The widow opened her hand to find two silver coins resting in her palm. "Sir, this is far too much!"

"No, 'tis not; we are taking your helper as well as your horse and this is a just payment for what you are giving."

"Thank you, kind Sir, and Godspeed."

Aedan had heard the conversation and had gone to saddle the horse. His plan was to ride without stopping for the half day journey back to the village. There he would take time only to change horses and be off to Iar Connaught. He hoped Ronan and Caolyn had not had time to be alone together and their journey did not find Ronan asking to formally court Caolyn.

Fiona came running from the house in time to see the transaction made for the horse. She ran to the widow, hugged and thanked her for everything. "Go, Fiona, I pray that you will be blessed with family that loves you. Remember to stay brave as you have been. You will be missed." Fiona separated from the widow and went to the waiting horse. Aedan helped her up and the three were off.

Fortunately the weather was on their side and the road was a fairly well traveled and kept one. Aedan's greatest concern was that Drest, more than Fiona, would slow his pace.

"Drest," Aedan began, "Please forgive any discourteous words I may impart. I fear that I could make greater haste on my own. Do you feel that you and Fiona could make it back to the village on your own before the sun sets this day?"

"My thought, exactly, Lad. Be off, you can make greater advance on your own. Fiona, do you feel safe with this old warrior at your side?"

"Sir Drest, I have long fended for myself," Fiona responded. "I have kept animals away from my door when I was with me Da and I can defend myself against the human animal as well."

Drest and Aedan could both see that Fiona was a strong and determined young woman. It was clear that she knew her own mind and she had been made strong by the life she endured with a drunkard father.

"Go, Aedan, we will be fine. We will make the village well before dark. As you have seen today, I still have a bit of warrior stock left in these old bones. Off with you now, take care to make haste, and let Cynara and all know of what we have learned. This changes everything."

"Aye, it most surely does. I am off then. Stick to the main road and you will be fine. When you arrive at the village, take Fiona to the House and seek audience with Lady Ava. She should be made aware of these happenings." Aedan turned to go and in a moment his steed was galloping at full speed.

"We will take care of each other, Sir Drest," Fiona commented. "Be at ease. I will not slow our pace. I am of strong and competent stock."

"Of that I have no doubt, Mistress Fiona," Drest said with a smile. "Come, we go to the village."

XXXVI

Aedan knew that a normal pace would take him half a day to complete. He also knew that his steed could be pushed to the limit and he could make the village in half the time. He dug his heels into the horse's side and pushed him on. If he could be at the village in three hours, he could stop long enough to change horses.

He was busy processing all this in his mind while he was remembering that Ronan, Caolyn and the others had started a little while ahead of them on the day that they left. It would take nearly a full day to get to Nora's homestead and they would spend the night making plans to carry out the task of fixing the wish. If he were correct, that would mean that they would most likely be starting out on this morn to go to the Wishing Stone. He knew that there was no way he could get to them before the task was completed. But then, his hope was to get to them before Ronan formally asked to court Caolyn and before any harmful things happened to taint their affections and reputations. This would not bode well with the Chieftain. Lady Ava might be forced to ban Caolyn from the house. They would become outcasts.

He would have to trust that Drest would offer

substantial explanation of all that they had learned, and that, if the gods deemed it so, all would be made right.

He thought of Ronan. He loved him like a brother, and yet Ronan did not confide in him. How could he not explain that he had a sister and a father? He could understand that Ronan must have been ashamed of his sire, but to leave his sister there... "If nothing else, we have rescued Fiona from an unpleasant fate," he thought.

His thoughts turned to Caolyn, "I never let my feelings for her show. I could not vie for Caolyn's affection when it was clear that Ronan had feelings for her. What will come of all this? Will they believe me when I make them aware of all we have learned?"

So much was going through his mind that he did not notice the blackening of the sky. "Shades be damned!" he shouted. "I do not need a storm rising. I do not need anything to slow my pace." The clouds were so full and black and seemed as if they were touching the ground, and yet, there was no wind. "What is happening?"

Suddenly, the clouds opened and the vision before him was that of a beautiful woman. She looked to be Caolyn, but it could not be. He stopped and stared and waited. The vision opened her arms and pointed toward a thicket. "Go, a fresh steed awaits you. In the sack he carries, find a map that will bring you to the area of Iar Connaught. This map is not of any road. You must follow it exactly, and you will be at the place of the Wishing Stone in time. Then, you will be able to aid my daughter and your friends."

Aedan was stunned and did not understand how this could be. "Lady, how can I believe you? I do not know you."

"I am Caolyn's mother. I have been granted permission by the Great Goddess to come to her aid. She must survive this journey. She must make the wish right and then go on to perfect her craft. Her knowledge will be needed by the House. Make haste to save her and the group. You must trust that this is so. I must leave; my time is up. Go, Aedan and tell her I am with her always."

Aedan was about to speak again, but the clouds parted and the sun shone high in the sky. He followed the vision's instructions and went to the thicket. There, indeed was a glorious mount; the finest steed he had ever seen. He had a magnificent flowing mane and he was black as the midnight sky. Aedan also noticed that he was strong and sleek; he was surely he was built for fast travel. As the vision stated, the horse carried a sack and in it a map the likes of which he had never seen.

He called his mount to him and removed the bridle. From the sacks on the saddle he took a few personal things including his broad sword. On a piece of parchment, he scratched out, "Have no fear. I am well." He placed the parchment under the saddle and slapped the horse's end shouting, "Be off to the village!"

Aedan went back to the beautiful horse, and mounted. "Well, my fine steed, we are off." The horse reared up and sped in the direction of Iar Connaught. It was as if he already knew the way.

They had not traveled very far when the steed came to a sudden halt. In front of them was an odd-looking growth, a huge mass of brown and grey twigs and brambles. It was about the height of a hut and as wide as well. It seemed to have grown into a circular shape. It was like nothing Aedan had seen before. Aedan tried to nudge the horse forward, but he would not move. He tried to dismount, but the horse reared up and moved backwards. Frustrated, Aedan took out the map and tried to interpret the drawing.

The map was full of various landmarks and arrows showing North, South, East and West. There on the map was a drawing that resembled the bush. Beneath the bush were the words, "Whistle like the red breasted bird." Aedan scratched his head and said to the horse, "Am I to whistle like a bird? I am not sure I know his song." Suddenly, atop the bush, was a red breasted bird, chirping for all he was worth. Aedan listened and imitated as best he could. On the first try the horse snorted and pawed the ground. "Aye, not too good is it?" He tried again and this time he felt the ground rumble and saw the bush shake. Aedan felt his warrior senses tensing, but in a moment the branches parted and there was a large gaping hole big enough for them to enter.

It took Aedan a moment to collect his senses, and he placed his hand on the hilt of a small knife he kept in his boot. He looked around. All was quiet, the bird was gone, and he was alone again with the horse. Before Aedan could even slap the reins to move the horse, he was off in a shot. They were inside the bush.

It was dark only for a moment and then the road seemed to be lit with candles lighting the way. Overhead, he saw what appeared to be the wall of a cave. They were traveling downward at a speed that Aedan had never experienced before. The horse was sure footed and seemed to know his way, just like any stray horse returning to his home stall. Aedan decided to let the horse be in charge and wait for the next moment that he would need to consult the map.

Karyn Finneron

XXXVII

As the group departed from Nora's family homestead, the sun was well above the horizon. If the sunny day held its promise they would have ample time to get to the Wishing Stone and be well on their way back to the village.

Ronan was busy mulling over possible scenarios in his head. He wanted to have as many planned preparations of escape as possible. He was still troubled by his dreams and his concerns over dangers that could not be seen or anticipated. He was riding ahead of the wagon that was carrying Nora, Caolyn and Cynara. Brian was managing the wagon, staying alert and aware of his surroundings. Paidric was bringing up the rear on his own mount.

It was not long before they were near the area of the Stone. Ronan brought the group to a halt and rode back to the wagon. "Brian, Padriac come, let us go over our stations for when we arrive at the site of the Stone."

The three men gathered together and discussed the plan. In the wagon Nora, Caolyn and Cynara formed a circle. "Nora, have you seen anything foreboding about?" Cynara inquired.

"Nay, nothing as yet, Cynara. I am trying to keep thoughts from my skull. I need to be clear headed, but pieces of the vision that I saw keep trying to enter my thoughts."

"Let the thoughts come, Child. Do not be afraid. They may be helpful to you in some way or perhaps they will foster another vision to come." Cynara placed a comforting arm around Nora, "You have been a great help and blessing to us thus far. Your gift of fey may be beneficial for us yet again."

Nora just nodded and smiled at Cynara.

"Caolyn, have you been rehearsing the words of the wishing spell? You must not say them aloud until you are ready to toss the stone! The more the words are set out, the less power they have when they are needed."

Caolyn looked at Cynara and in her most confident voice responded, "Yes Auntie, I am ready." Cynara could see in Caolyn's eyes that, she was not as confident, as her voice sounded.

"You will do well, Caolyn. Have no fear. Nora's vision has foretold that you will have Banba and all of her might as a warrior goddess to protecting you, along with the spirit of your mother. You must draw on that strength. It will carry you through your task. You must believe in yourself. You have the ability and spirit to do this!"

"I will Auntie, I will not let you down, I……"

"No, child, you will not betray what the Goddess has bestowed on you and, you will not let yourself down!" Cynara was as forceful as she felt she could be without making Caolyn more fearful.

Ronan dismounted and went to the women in the wagon. "We are ready. Ladies. Are you also prepared?"

"Aye, let this task be finished," Cynara replied.

"Good, now, when we get to the site of the Stone,

Brai, Nora and Cynara will stay back with the wagon. Cynara, you will have sight of the Stone and the giant's hand. I will take Caolyn with me on the horse and bring her to the Stone. I will stay close enough to snatch her away if I feel there is danger. Paidric will be on a small knoll above the hand but hidden in the thickets and trees. He will be ready to alert Brian to turn the wagon in order to make haste to leave. Then, if all is well, he will then join you. Do you all understand?"

Cynara spoke for the group. "We will be at the ready, and I have brought herbs that make a thick smoke to give us the ability to escape a short distance without being seen. It may be helpful if we have to run."

"I will leave that to you, Cynara. I have great faith and trust in your instincts. We will all have to be at our best. We must hope that we have the power of all that is holy with us! Let us then be off and make haste to complete this business. The sooner we can be away the better!" Ronan turned and went back to the front of the wagon, and the little group moved on toward the final piece of road leading to the Stone.

XXXVIII

Aedan was speeding through the tunnel, and the great steed was in no need of guidance or direction from him. Soon they came to a massive iron gate, which was covered with overgrown brambles and vines. The horse stopped suddenly again, nearly tossing Aedan off his back. "Ho there, Great Steed, I have no interest in being tossed to the ground! What am I to do now, my friend? The growth on the gate is so thick that it will take too long to cut through. Can you not jump the gate?"

The great horse pawed the ground, but no matter how Aedan tried he would not back up to attempt a jump. "Back to the map," Aedan said aloud. He took the map and uncurled it. There on the parchment was a picture of the gate. Next to the gate the words 'Call for the wee man' were scrawled. "The wee man," Aedan, thought scratching his head. There was no name to be called, out so Aedan in his loudest voice called "WEE MAN, COME!"

The words were no sooner out of his mouth when from the overgrowth on the gate appeared a dwarf. He was very old, as well as, very small. With the exception of the lavender cap tilted on his head, he was dressed in the colors of the woods. "Ye dina' have to shout. I be not deaf!" the little man said. "What is your pleasure, sir. It must be of great importance for I see you are riding Enbarr, the steed of the great and powerful Mannin Mac Lir."

"What, the god of the land and sea, the powerful magician? This is his steed!?" Aedan could not believe his ears. He nearly fell of the horse with the news.

"Aye, Sir, you have been given a great gift. Do ye know that Enbarr can travel land and sea at great speed? You must not abuse this gift."

"Well, Wee One, I have let this great steed take me along. I am at the mercy of his knowing the way. I cannot tarry. I am to help my friends in lar Connaught. Help me get through the gate, please."

The little man just laughed. "Silly human, do ye not know that, in the land under the land, time stands still? When you get to lar Connaught you will find that no time has passed. You will arrive in time to help your friends. Be assured that Enbarr will achieve the task he has been sent to do."

The little man moved to the iron gate, and with a touch of his hand the overgrown bush receded. He then reached into his lavender hat and took out a great silver key to unlock the gate. The gate opened wide with ease. "Be on your way now, Sir. There is to be a great battle between the giant of legend and your friends. Do not fear. Listen to Enbarr. Let him take and guide you to where you will be of most assistance."

"Thank you, Wee Man, uh, do you have a name, sir?" Aedan asked, embarrassed that he had not asked the kindly man before.

"Aye, it be Murt, but no bother. Once you are back above it will be erased from your memory as will be the path that you took. You will remember riding Enbarr, for that is always unforgettable. You can tell your children and their children how you were once favored by the gods. Now go, Aedan, your destiny awaits."

Aedan passed through the gate and turned to thank Murt, but he was no longer there and the gate was gone as well. He turned back in the saddle and Enbarr was off.

Aedan had little to do other than to hold tightly to the reins and keep himself upright in the saddle. Enbarr was speeding along the path that seemed to be made of clouds. The roadway was white as snow and stirred up easily with the pounding of Enbarr's hooves.

It wasn't long before Aedan thought he could hear water rushing above them. "We must be nearing the end of the tunnel and then we will be above the ground," he thought. He no sooner finished the thought when he could feel Enbarr starting to climb up hill. The hill seemed steep, and yet the great horse never slowed or tired. At the crest of the hill, Enbarr stopped and whinnied. Aedan did not know what to do next. Again, he referred to the map as the sound of rushing water grew louder. Perhaps the tunnel was filling with water? This thought set his warrior senses on alert.

On the map there was a drawing of a hill, which he took to be the point that they had come to be on. Atop of the drawing of the hill was an arrow, pointing up and above the arrow there appeared to be waves or a river. Now, the sound of rushing water was almost deafening. He looked up and could see water rushing above him but there did not seem to be a way through. "By the gods, Enbarr, how will we escape? Are you able to free us from the tunnel?"

Enbarr reared up on his hind legs and came down, pawing the ground with his great hooves, and the water above flowed down over the huge steps of a water fall. Aedan yelled in shock and in fear. "How, Noble Steed will we get to the top?" Without hesitation, Enbarr climbed the flowing, silver falls of water and, in what seemed like an instant, they were out of the tunnel.

Aedan shouted for joy while rubbing the massive neck of Enbarr. "By the gods, you are magnificent! I am ever in your debt, Enbarr. Now I trust you know the way to my friends?"

Enbarr shook his head, pawed the ground and sped toward his destination.

XXXIX

At Iar Connaught, the group was now ready for their task. Ronan was mounted on his horse in a place that gave him a full view of the Wishing Stone. He could also clearly see Brian, Nora and Cynara in the wagon. Caolyn moved toward the stone from where Ronan had allowed her to dismount. He looked around for Padriac and found him on a knoll slightly above where the giant's stone hand rested on the ground.

As Ronan was getting his bearings and taking in the full view of the area, he had a moment of fear. This was the first chance any of them had to be near the Stone or the hand. The Stone was massive. Would Caolyn be strong enough to toss the stone carrying the wish over the peak? She needed strength, but she needed to be on the mark as well. With her back to the Stone and tossing the wish over would be no easy feat. He knew Caolyn to be strong, and he was grateful that her good height would be helpful, but the task in this moment seemed daunting.

Then, there was the hand. It was indeed massive. It had turned black over the years, which also made it more threatening in appearance. It was at least eight warrior's hands high and four hands wide. Ronan shuddered at the thought of the giant rising from the earth, as some of the legends had foretold. He wanted to shout to Caolyn to hurry, but he also knew he must not cause her any fear. She had enough on her mind already. "By the gods, make me brave and make this day become the past in great haste! Caolyn's mother, if your spirit be about, and if Banba is at your side, I invoke you both to be at our aid."

Caolyn had reached the base of the Stone. In her right hand she held a stone from the land in the area of the lough. Ronan knew that the stone she held was wrapped in a basil leaf with the name of Brenna's warrior inscribed on it. The leaf had been bound to the stone with a piece of fabric from Brenna's garments and tied tightly with Brenna's hair. "Strange," he thought. "I never asked the name of the warrior Brenna desires. Perhaps,, it is best I do not know. The less I know of spells and wishes the better off I may be. I am a warrior. I deal with matters of physical protection and defense of the defenseless. Matters of the spirit realm I know little of and I have no desire to know more."

A gust of wind chilled him. And once again he was on the alert though nothing around him seemed to be out of the ordinary.

Caolyn began to speak.

Goddess Caolainn hear my plea
I have made a wish that cannot be
I did not heed the teachings bestowed upon me
So now this wish I remedy
I set a name upon this basil leaf
The stone is bound with her garment sleek

Suddenly, the ground shook. The land rippled as if in waves. Ronan looked about. Nothing else seemed out of place, and yet things were not as they had been a moment before. Nora, who was now wailing, was standing and rocking in the wagon. Cynara stood as well keeping Brian away from Nora so that her vision would not be disturbed. Cynara screamed, "Continue, Caolyn! Make haste! Do not waiver. Complete the spell!"

Caolyn was holding the stone. Her face was white as chalk. Ronan recognized fear when he saw it. He had seen it before on the faces of young warriors in their first battle. His first instinct was to ride and snatch up Caolyn, but he held his ground. If she completed the spell before there were any other unnatural happenings, he would still have time to gather her up.

Caolyn began again in a loud voice;

Reverse the wish I asked of thee
Return things back to what was past
I your namesake will honor thee
This I ask from above for below
As over the Wishing Stone I make my throw

As Caolyn released the stone, Ronan held his breath. All eyes watched the stone rise higher and higher. Just as it reached the peak and started over, Padriac began to let out a cheer. At the same time, the ground began to move again, and Nora was screamed "The Hand, The Hand!"

The hand seemed to be trying to wrestle itself free from the ground. Ronan spurred the horse toward Caolyn while shouting "Padriac, to the wagon, Brian, be at the ready!" Caolyn started running towards Ronan when a finger of the hand stretched out and wrapped around her ankle. "NO!" Caolyn shouted. Ronan moved faster but the hand seemed to have speed of its own.

Padriac changed direction and ran to assist Ronan. With his knife he stabbed the finger wrapped around Caolyn's ankle. The knife snapped in two as if it were a twig. Padriac then began pounding the tightly wrapped finger.

Ronan now had his sword drawn and was attempting to cut at the giant's hand. Every time he struck the hand, it was if he were slashing at air. There was no impact. Somewhere, in the background, Ronan could hear what sounded like battle cries. The sky darkened. A storm was coming. "By the gods," Ronan thought, "can we not have a bit of luck this day!"

Brian screamed at Ronan, "The lake, it is swirling! It cannot be. There comes a rider on a great horse; the steed comes across the water at great speed."

Ronan could not take his eyes away from the giant's hand. Caolyn was tiring from trying to wrench herself free from the giant. Ronan noticed that her foot was turning blue from the tight grasp on her ankle. He knew he was losing ground.

Suddenly Nora screamed again, "I see Banba and Myra; they are telling us to believe. We will be safe soon!"

No sooner had the words left Nora's mouth, when the horse and rider were there at Ronan's side. "Aedan, by heavens, how!"

The great horse reared up and slammed down his powerful hooves on the giant's hand. Still the hand held fast. He reared again and this time Ronan and Aedan both struck at the same time as the horse's hooves came down with a mighty blow. The finger holding Caolyn's ankle was smashed nearly flat. Caolyn's foot was greatly discolored, and she had lost consciousness. Aedan dismounted the great horse and ran to Caolyn. He rolled her on to her back and lifted her from the ground.

Suddenly the darkness disappeared and the sun came out. The ground was no longer trembling. The giant's hand now lay flat with the marks of Enbarr's great hooves imbedded into it.

There was great cheering among the group. Cynara shouted, "Make haste! Bring Caolyn, so that I may tend to her. We must be away! There will be time for rejoicing once we are far from this land of mystery."

Aedan brought Caolyn to the wagon and laid her gently inside. "Aedan, you were granted a ride on the great horse of Mannin Mac Lir! Enbarr, 'tis been a long while since we met," Cynara said as she gave Enbarr an apple. Enbarr shook his mane and pawed the ground. "Come we must be away from this place. Caolyn and Nora need tending and we all need rest."

Aedan turned to Enbarr, and nuzzled his nose and patted his neck. "Thank you, Great Enbarr. I will never forget you and how you rescued my friends. I will spend my days honoring your name and that of Manan Mac Lir." Enbarr reared up and whinnied. Before another word was spoken, he turned, and in an instant, was gone.

XL

The small group turned away from the Wishing Stone, and the giant's mangled hand. It would be a long time, if ever, before the hand would resemble what it had been. For a few moments, as the wagon moved away, the only sounds were the wind gently blowing and birdsong. The sky was beautiful, an array of clouds, sun streaked with pinks and gold. The wretched weather, and trembling of the ground that surrounded the place, while Caolyn was making the wish, seemed as if it had never happened.

Everyone was lost in thought, trying to make sense of all that had occurred, except for Caolyn and Nora. They were still somewhere lost in a state of unconsciousness.

Finally, the silence was broken by Cynara. "Ronan, I do not think we can journey back to the village. Caolyn's wounds need more tending than what I can do here in the wagon. I feel it would be best to take refuge with Nora's Mam again."

"Aye, I have been thinking on that as well. We are all to the point of exhaustion, and the sun will be nearly set by the time we reach Nora's home. I fear a night on the road would make for a bad decision."

Cynara nodded in agreement, and in that moment,

Nora awoke calling out to Caolyn and flailing her arms about wildly. "Hush," Cynara began. "We are all safe. Caolyn is hurt, but she will mend. We are going back to your home. You did well, Child."

"In my vision, I could see the giant reaching for Caolyn. I tried to warn her! Her leg, her leg!" Nora was crying inconsolably.

"Shhh, Child, here drink this lavender and chamomile water. It is all I have here, but it will help calm you until we get to your home." Cynara brought the cup to Nora's lips, who drank as if she had not had a sip for days. Then Cynara wrapped her in a blanket, and had her lie down. "Rest now. We will soon be home. Do not fret over Caolyn. She is strong and she will heal."

Ronan turned to Padric, and gave him orders to make haste to his home so that his mam could prepare the house for another night. "Be sure to advise her that Caolyn is injured and will need tending. Your sister may also need to be comforted and kept calm. We will all need rest, and some strong ale or spirits would be of great help."

"Aye, Ronan, me Mam is very good with tending to hurts. She has also been known to have a bit of strong drink about for doctoring." Padric kicked his heels into his mount and was gone.

Aedan and Ronan were now left to each other's company. "Aedan, by the gods, how did you manage to find us? Where did you get the great horse? I thought you were at the village. Who sent you to save us?"

"My friend, 'tis a long story, and I have much to tell you. This much I will say; Drest set out to find Caolyn's sire. The Chieftain did not want the old warrior to go it alone, and so he gave me leave to accompany him. The rest of the story will have to wait until we can be seated, and Caolyn as well as Cynara must be part of the telling."

Just as Aedan finished speaking, Nora's home came into sight. They could see Padriac and Margaret running toward the wagon.

"My Girl! my Girl!" Margaret was shouting.

"Have no fear," Cynara said, standing in the wagon. "She has served us well, and she will be fine. There is nothing wrong that a hot meal, and a good night's rest cannot fix."

The wagon came to a stop in front of the homestead. Caolyn was stirring, but did not awake. Aedan and Ronan went to the wagon to assist Cynara in getting both girls down. Ronan jumped inside and lifted Caolyn as if she were a doll. Ronan handed her down to Aedan. He took her in his arms, and lovingly held her as she rested her head on his chest. Ronan could not mistake the look on Aedan's face as he took her. He had seen the face of one in love before.

Ronan silently climbed down from the wagon, and though only think only of returning to the village. He had a sudden urge to talk to the Chieftain about Brenna.

XLI

Once everyone was inside the homestead Cynara, Margaret and Nora set about making Caolyn comfortable. Margaret began to cook a meal for all. Nora sat by Caolyn's side holding her hand and gently speaking to her, though she remained unresponsive. Cynara was prepared healing herbs to use with cool wraps for the badly bruised foot and also a strong potion for pain. She knew once Caolyn was fully awake the pain would begin.

"She will have much pain when she wakes," Cynara thought. "I need to get a better feel for the wound, but I would rather she wake from her slumber on her own. I hope there are no bones to mend, but that will have to wait until I can lay my hands upon the leg and foot."

Cynara's thoughts were broken by Margaret's voice. "Come along, Cynara, you must eat and rest before the poor girl wakes. You too, Nora, Caolyn is within our sight. We will tend to her once she wakens. Both of you need to be refreshed and ready for that happening. I will sit with her while you both refresh yourselves."

Nora and Cynara went to the hearth and ate the simple meal of bread and root vegetable stew. They both found their hunger to be greater than realized. There was little conversation because they were lost in their own thoughts.

Outside, Ronan, Aedan, along with the boys, were busy tending to the horses and unpacking the wagon. The mood was somber, and though there was much to be said, for a few moments all was quiet.

"Padriac, might you go to see if your mam may have a bit of food for us to sup and something to quench our thirst?" Ronan said.

"Aye, Ronan, she has set out cups by the hearth for stew, and she has placed a jug of ale with the food. Brian, come along, you can help me carry the food."

Brian nearly flew off his feet; he was trying hard not to show his concern for Nora, but he needed to see if she was more herself. He was frightened for her with all that she had experienced that day, and any chance to set his mind at ease was a welcome chance.

As the two younger men departed, Ronan and Aedan sat staring at each other. Neither one of them wanted to be the first to break the deafening silence that surrounded them.

Finally, Ronan began, "Aedan, pray now will you explain how you came to be with us! I was feeling that all hope was lost, and then there you were, like a god, on the great horse! How did….."

"Aye, Ronan, there is much to be told about all that has happened. I believe we each have a story to tell. Perhaps it is best if you begin. At least we both have some knowledge of your journey and its purpose. My part in the story will be told in due time. I am hoping to tell it in the company of Caolyn and Cynara, as well as you, for it will have meaning for all."

"As you know, Aedan, the Chieftain asked that I

accompany Caolyn and the group to lar Cannaught in order to set this blasted wish right. Even after meeting with Lady Ava and hearing that the area was a mystical land full of legend and strange happenings, I believed, my talents as a warrior were being used for folly. Because of my attachment to Caolyn, I was prepared to go, if for no other reason than to be near her and to find favor with Cynara. I planned to ask to court her, but there was never a good time before the wishing ceremony and now...." Ronan was hanging his head and shaking it as if to send off any feelings for all that had happened.

"What say you, my friend, are you befuddled, sorrowful, what is it?"

"Aedan, I am empty. I don't feel the same way about Caolyn as I did when we started on the journey. My feelings have changed. I admire her, and I want in some way to be in her life, but something is not as it was before."

"Perhaps," Aedan began.

"Ronan, Aedan, come, Caolyn is waking!" Brian called from the house.

The two warriors rose and went to the house. Once inside, it was clear that Cynara was in charge. She had made a mound of fresh straw and placed it near the hearth. On the bed of straw were herbs and sweet lavender, as well as a homespun blanket that held Caolyn in a gentle wrap. She was drifting back and forth between the sleep of the ill and painful wakefulness.

"Come, Ronan, sit here by Caolyn. She has been calling your name," Cynara said as she motioned to Ronan.

Ronan appeared embarrassed by the invitation. "Perhaps it is best if I stay aside, Mistress."

Just then, Caolyn woke again and called out for Ronan. "Are ye about, Ronan? Did I not hear your voice? Are you safe, unhurt?"

Ronan walked stiffly to Caolyn's side and took her hand without nodding or kneeling to comfort her. "I am here, brave girl. Are ye well?"

There was a hush in the room, as it was duly noted, that Ronan's actions seemed a bit queer. The looks on the faces of those gathered almost seemed to be inquiring if Ronan was daft. All but, Cynara--she knew by Ronan's actions that the wish had worked. The spell was broken. His concern for Caolyn was not one of a man wanting to be handfasted to the young woman in front of him, but rather one of general concern for a companion who had suffered a misfortune.

"I am better now, knowing that you are safe. I can never thank the Goddess enough for putting you there with me to rescue and protect me. I owe you my life."

"Nay, Caolyn, it was merely the duty of a warrior sent on a task to protect the group. Look, Aedan is here as well. There would be no rescue if he had not arrived in time to assist with the task. Come, Aedan, come and see that we have been successful. Caolyn is well."

Aedan went to the mound of straw and dropped to his knees to be closer to Caolyn. He gently took her hand in his and held back the urge to kiss it. He reminded himself this was not the time, even though everything inside him was screaming for him to gather her up in his arms. He wanted to protect her from all that might harm her. "Does the foot pain you much? You were so brave. I wish I could have been there more quickly. I have much to tell you and everyone...."

"Enough, Aedan," Cynara interrupted. "There will

be time on the morrow for talk. We must let her rest. All of you find where you will be settled for the night." Cynara went to Caolyn and made her drink a cup of tea that had foxglove for pain and honeyed mead for sleep. "Rest now, my girl, you have been made aware that all of us are fine. The task is done and the wish is made right. Do you understand what you have accomplished?"

Caolyn nodded. Cynara rubbed Caolyn's cheek, wiping away the tear that had escaped her eye. Cynara could tell by the look in Caolyn's eyes that she knew Ronan was now lost to her as a mate.

Cynara left Caolyn's side and went to the two warriors. "Go and start a fire. Eat your sup and, I will be along to discuss and sort out the happenings of this day."

"Aye," both young men said in unison and departed to do Cynara's bidding.

XLII

Cynara found both warriors sitting by the fire and finishing the remains of their meal. As she approached, they both stood to greet her. "Sit, my brave ones," she began, "we have much to discuss this night. First, let me commend you both for your bravery. There were moments when I felt all would be lost and, perhaps, if Aedan had not arrived, the outcome would have not gone in our favor. Pray tell us how you came to be of assistance?"

"Mistress, not long after you all set out on your journey, Sir Drest asked the Chieftain to take his leave of the village. He was on a mission to find Caolyn's sire, and to see if he could set things right. The Chieftain did not want him to go it alone, and I was thus assigned to accompany him. At first, he merely said he was seeking an old warrior friend, but along the way he made his true reason known to me."

"And did he find Caolyn's sire?"

"Indeed, and that is not the only thing we found in our search." Aedan looked toward Ronan who did not appear at all interested in Drest's journey to find Caolyn's sire.

"The old warrior he wished to find is most likely gone to the otherworld," Ronan thought.

"Go on, Sir," Cynara requested. She had a feeling that something important was about to be revealed.

"Ronan," Aedan began, "know that I love you like a brother. I truly had no idea when we set out that, we would discover something of your family."

"Aedan, of what do you speak? Out with it! Do not keep us in the dark!"

"My friend, Caolyn is… she is, your half- sister. You have the same sire!"

Ronan jumped to his feet and started toward Aedan. "Liar!" he shouted. "This cannot be! Me da sired Caolyn?"

Cynara swiftly spoke. "Ronan, sit down! You know that Caolyn has no family. Let me speak of her history."

Cynara told the story of Myra meeting a warrior named Bain at a Beltane feast. She described his looks, and explained he was not from the village. She told how Drest went to find him when Myra was with child, but found that Bain was already bound to another, and had children as well.

Ronan had his head in his hands. He realized that the Bain of whom they spoke and his sire were one and the same. The description he had heard was that of his father. As he thought about this, he realized that he was not upset that Caolyn was his sister. Since the incident at the Stone, he knew that his feelings for her had changed. He did not understand why, but now, at least, he had a reason to know why there could be no feelings of being bound to each other. It would be forbidden.

Aedan began to tell the story of how he came to find the group at the Stone. He also told Ronan that they had taken his sister Fiona away from his sire. Drest had taken her on to the House of Maidens.

"I apologize for gaps in my story," Aedan continued. "I had a vision of Caolyn's mother that told me the Goddess had allowed her to come to me. This vision told me where I would find Enbarr. I was given a map, but I cannot remember how I came upon all of you. I do remember Enbarr climbing a great water fall and then we were there to help all of you. Strange, that I cannot remember it all."

"You cannot remember, Aedan," Cynara began, "because the wee man that you met in the land under the earth took back your memory. He guards the secrets of the god Arwen, Enbarr's master."

"Cynara," Ronan began, "can you explain everything about the wish now that it has been made right? Why were so many warriors affected by the wish, and I did not seem to be?"

"Because, Ronan, when Caolyn made the wish for Brenna, she did not have the name of the warrior that Brenna desired. When she made the wish at the well, she inscribed on the basil leaf 'Brenna's warrior.' It appears that there were many in the village who desired to be Brenna's warrior."

"But then, what about me?" Aedan asked.

Cynara chuckled, "dear Boy, you were already smitten. Somethings even the gods cannot change."

Aedan was blushing from head to toe. Ronan gave him a friendly punch on the arm. "Aye and now you will have to have my permission to court her!"

"Now that this is settled," Cynara said, "we will have to be mindful of Caolyn's injuries, and if possible, we will begin our return to the village on the morrow."

"How bad do you think her injuries are, Mistress?" Aedan asked.

"I do not think the bones are damaged, but she will have a lot of bruising and swelling for a time. I can use herbs to ease the pain and reduce swelling, but with rest she should be fine in due time. Now we must all put this day behind us and be ready to depart in the morning, if Caolyn can make the journey."

"When do you think we should tell her about all we have come to know of her family?" Ronan inquired.

"If she is well in the morning, we may tell her together. Surrounded by friends, and family, will ease the telling. Good night, Dear warriors. Take your rest." Cynara turned and headed for the house.

The two young warriors were left standing together. "Ronan, sit, I have a bit more to tell you. When I accompanied Drest to the village where he went in years past, he told me about all that he did to have your sire do right by his sister. He wanted revenge, but Myra would not have it. She told him that her babe could be raised in the House. When we heard that Bain, your da, lived alone and that he had given his life over to the drink, we had concerns that Drest would not be able to speak with him. We were also told about Fiona and how she had fled his home and fostered herself to a widow. He went after her, Ronan, in a way that….."

"Stop, this is my sorrow to bear! I wanted to take her with me, but a warrior's life is not one that can sustain a maid. She would not have me give up my life. I returned from time to time to give her money, food and to repair the hut. I did not think he would ever hurt her."

Ronan sat with his head buried in his hands. Aedan let his friend have the time he needed, and then Ronan spoke again.

"I have never had much love for me da. He beat me

and me ma. It was she that bade me to leave for fear that one of us would kill the other. I was away when she went on to the otherworld. My peace is in knowing it was a fever and not a beating that took her from us. I wonder how Caolyn will feel when she realizes that we are kin and that her Da is a horrible excuse for a man."

"Well, my friend, if she takes the news in the same manner as Fiona did, she will dance for joy, injured foot or not."

Ronan smiled. "I am not like him, Aedan. Me ma made sure that she taught me well. She taught me respect, honor and kindness. I honor her memory by practicing these. I may have failed Fiona, but now that she is away from that wretch, I can care for her."

"Come Ronan, we must bed down for the night. We do not know what the morrow brings, but it surely must have more favor than this day."

XLIII

Morning came far too quickly for the exhausted group, but the sun rose in beautiful shades of gold and burnt henna. It truly was going to be a beautiful day.

"Ho, Ronan, are ye awake? 'Tis a fine sunrise you are missing."

"Aye, my friend, I am awake, but truth be told, I would prefer to stay here and sleep the day away."

"Well," Aedan began, "I would like to do the same, but it is time to make for the village. If we get a decent start we should be there before night fall. We have much to do to prepare. What say ye to getting up before the house, and make a start on readying the wagon and the horses?"

"Aye, we will be quiet and let the house rest as long as possible. I am sure Cynara will be about giving orders for preparations before long."

The two comrades got up and went to the well to wash and gather water for the horses. They filled the necessary water skins for the journey back to the village. Aedan set about gathering fresh hay for Caolyn to lie on during the journey. He was thinking about her and wondering how the night had been within the house. He knew she had the best care with Cynara as her provider. He felt useless with regards to offering any assistance, but at least he could make the wagon as comfortable as possible.

It wasn't long before there were stirrings in the house. Padriac and Brian woke soon after they heard their friends moving around in the barn, ministering to the horses. "Good morn, Ronan and Aedan," Brian greeted them. "Are we readying for the journey home?"

"Aye, Brian," Ronan answered. "The more we ready ourselves now the sooner we can be on the road. We will break fast as soon as Mistress Margaret bids us enter the house."

"Good, I am ready to return. This journey has taught me much, and I feel I have become wiser for it. I have you to thank for allowing me to come."

"No need for thanks, Brian. You were of great assistance. I could not have held off the Giant's hand without Padriac. Knowing you were on the ready to save Caolyn was one thing for which I did not have cause to worry. You have both proven yourselves to be brave and loyal comrades."

Brian smiled and thanked Ronan. He then was off to the barn to finish packing the wagon and to ready the horse.

Ronan looked toward the homestead just as Cynara was coming out. She waved and called the young men into break fast.

Once inside the door, they found Caolyn sitting on a chair with her injured foot resting on a mound of fresh hay. She appeared to be quite comfortable and well. "Come, come," Cynara began. "Gather round the table. Margaret and Nora have prepared a fine meal for us. We will be well sustained for the travel."

"Good morn, Caolyn," Aedan began. "Are ye well?"

"Yes, Aedan, and I believe that we all have you to thank for finishing off the evil in the Giant's hand and for helping to rescue the lot of us. For this, I offer my thanks."

"Caolyn, if it had not been for my ......"

"Aedan," Cynara interrupted. "Let us eat and then we will tell Caolyn of all that she has missed, and all that she needs to know before we depart. Come, enjoy what has been given to us by Margaret."

Everyone sat down and ate their meal of porridge with berries, fresh milk and newly baked brown bread slathered with butter. Once the meal was complete and things cleared away, Cynara moved closer to Caolyn. "Before we set out, my dear girl, there is much we have to tell you, but only if you are well enough to hear the story. Know that some of it may be disturbing to hear. Know, also, the story has had a peaceful and pleasant ending. Do you feel well enough?"

"Yes, Auntie, I want to know all that happened. I have so many questions, but I feel that I should have all of the story before I ask. Perhaps much will be answered in the telling."

"You have made a wise choice. Aedan, perhaps you should start with the journey you and Drest set out upon and what you have learned from the journey."

"May I sit closer to Caolyn?" Aedan asked.

"Of course, Aedan, come," Caolyn answered.

Aedan began. He told of Drest's desire to find Caolyn's sire. He told of the village they traveled to and of how they found her sire. When he got to the part where he revealed what Bain, her sire, was like; Caolyn's eyes began to fill with tears. Aedan took her hand and paused in the story. "Caolyn, I am sorry to hurt you in this way, but there is more."

"Go on," she responded.

"Caolyn, you and Ronan have the same sire. He is your brother!" The silence in the room was as heavy as wet wool. No one spoke for what seemed like an eternity.

"Ronan, come," Caolyn called.

Ronan went to her side and knelt down. "Is it true? You are my brother, my blood, my family?"

"Yes, I am your brother. Like you, I only found out after the day at the Wishing Stone. Our sire is a beastly man. I am not like him, Sister. I will honor and protect you as my family. There is one other thing. I, we, have a younger sister, Fiona. Drest has accompanied her to the House. She will be there to greet you."

Caolyn was now crying and hugging Ronan while still clasping Aedan's hand. "I cannot believe the good fortune that has come from a wish that was made wrong. We have all come through this challenge and are better for it. I am blessed."

The mood in the house was now one of celebration. The final preparations were made for the journey home. Soon everyone was ready. Caolyn and Cynara were comfortably seated in the wagon. Nora was hugging her mother good bye. Padriac and Brian were giving each other friendly shoves and barbs while discussing when they might see each other again. Brian helped Nora into the wagon. Margaret went to Brian with a stern warning to look after her girl. Cynara and Margaret hugged each other good bye. "We were blessed by the Goddess to have you here, Margaret. I cannot bear to think on what this journey would have been like without your care. May you be blessed."

"Aye, 'tis good that we have met. I know that Nora is in good and kind hands. May ye go with the gods and return if ye can. My home is yours as well."

"Come," Ronan called. "We must be away." Ronan took his place at the front of the wagon and Aedan at the back. The group moved on towards the east and the House and their village. Each was lost in his own thoughts. Some were thinking about their adventure and the stories they had to tell. Others were thinking of love and handfasting. As for Cynara, she was thinking of what had come to pass on this journey, what Caolyn had learned of her life and craft, and what the Lady Ava would think of all that happened. Lastly, she thought of going back to her home and wondering if Drest would journey with her.

Acknowledgements

I have so many wonderful, helpful people in my life, to not take a moment to acknowledge them would be a travesty. I had so much encouragement from friends, family and my writers group. To write a novel after writing primarily for young children was a reach. This book would not have come to fruition without them.

First, I want to thank my husband Barry for bringing me back to Ireland in 2017. This book was in its baby steps, and a visit to Kylemore Abbey in Co. Galway gave me inspiration to go on. You will understand why as you read the book.

Secondly, I thank my wonderful artists. Mary Nugent produced another wonderful cover for the book. This book also, for the first time, contains the art work of my oldest grandchild, Isabella. It is wonderful to see her name in print with mine. I am blessed.

Lastly, my wonderful friend, Elisabeth, volunteered her time to help me with the editing of the original manuscript. She was patient, kind, and if one can believe it; she made the editing fun.